Emily Andrews lives in
Seattle, Washington. Her poetry
has been published through the
International Library of Poetry
and Poetry.com, and featured on
one of their spoken albums. Her
interests include indie, punk rock
and industrial music, journaling
and old horror movies.

IN THE SAME SERIES

The Finer Points of Becoming Machine

EMILY ANDREWS

Ransom

The Finer Points of Becoming Machine

EMILY ANDREWS

Series Editor: Peter Lancett

Published by Ransom Publishing Ltd.
51 Southgate Street, Winchester, Hampshire SO23 9EH, UK
www.ransom.co.uk

ISBN 978 184167 714 9

First published in 2009
Copyright © 2009 Ransom Publishing Ltd.
Cover by Flame Design, Cape Town, South Africa

Firstly, I'd like to thank my friends and family for their love and support during the creation of this book, especially Victoria Lane, who introduced me to Peter Lancett and Ransom Publishing.

Special thanks to: my mother, Kyle, Jenna, my fathers, and my husband, who have in some way or another walked through each step of hell with me. Thank you for loving me, despite the fact that I am a complete mess.

A special thank you to Peter Lancett for his patience, knowledge, skill, and never ending support. You are an amazing writer and editor, and I am truly humbled as well as incredibly grateful to call you now my friend.

Lastly, I would like to dedicate this book to each and every person who has lived, died, or survived a life of abuse.

CHAPTER 1
'Can you feel, now?'

'Call 911. I did something really stupid,' are the last words I remember saying clearly. Whatever pills I had swallowed had begun to make me loopy, or maybe it was the bottle of Puerto Rican rum I had washed it down with, or hell, maybe it was from the blood loss as my arms streamed ribbons of ruby red. Either way though, the night takes on a nightmarish quality that leaves all but the major details hazy to me.

The day had started out normal enough. I woke up, and sighed in exhaustion at still breathing. I had gotten dressed in my usual outfit, black combat boots, black pants, black shirt, black sweater, heavy eyeliner. The vacant look in my eyes comes naturally now; I don't have to put that on anymore. I am sixteen years old. I am that weird kid in your class you whisper about and make fun of because she dresses in black and the few friends that she does have also dress in black and listen to depressing music while smoking cigarettes in the bathroom at lunch time.

My name is Emma, but that isn't important. This could be your story, the kid down the street's story, and in a way I wish it was; but it's not. It's mine, and mine alone to tell.

It was a fairly non-eventful day. Get on bus. Go to school. Ditch most of my classes. Smoke cigarettes. Get on bus, go back home. December 16th. The only reason I remember the day is because this is the day that shit hit the fan and I was forced to start dealing with all the crap in my head – or spend more time in a padded room than anyone should ever have to.

I had an older boyfriend named Donnie. He was a 21-year-old musician with bleached blond hair and beautiful features and looked *just* like the lead singer of my favorite band, which is probably the entire reason I loved him in the first place.

Anyways, school ends and he doesn't meet me like he was supposed to. A phone call a few hours later manages to tear my heart in two. 'You've got too many problems Emma. I'm sorry, I think we shouldn't be together any more.'

Looking back, it wasn't so much him that broke me. It was the fact that I poured what was left of my love and humanity into him and he, like everyone else in my life, hurt me. When I called my mom for condolence, she simply said, 'I'm sorry you're hurting,' but her voice told me the exact opposite. She didn't care either. Something bad and dark inside me clicks.

You see, I am the product of an abusive home, where violence, guilt and lies are a way of life. I grew up watching my mother get beaten black and blue, and eventually that happened to me as well. But I'll get to that a little later.

Anyways, after years of stuffing it in, hiding it, drowning myself in booze and drugs and sex in the vain attempt to forget the past, I had finally reached a breaking point. I was going to kill myself.

I put my favourite song on repeat, grabbed a butcher knife, emptied the medicine cabinet and crawled into the bathtub with a bottle of rum. 'One way or another, this is going to end,' I had told myself. I had scrawled the requisite suicide note but I couldn't think of anything to say, so all I said was that I was sorry.

I steel myself for this. Take a deep breath. Go. Slice ruby lines into porcelain skin. Swallow this bottle of pills. Chase it with rum. Repeat until finished. I don't know what made me get out of the tub and tell my grandma and little sister to call 911. But I did. And everything gets hazy after that.

Flashing lights and sirens. Emergency medical team working on me. And I was laughing, can you imagine? Laughing at the whole situation. It wasn't anywhere *near* funny, but somehow, it was all I could do.

Fade out.

Fade in to an ambulance and being strapped to a stretcher. I can feel my mascara running down my face. I think I am afraid, but I'm not entirely sure I can feel any more. My body is bones and skin and blood right now. I am wet and cold. I try to hold on to this paramedic's clothing, to feel something so I know that I am still here.

Fade out.

Fade into intravenous lines and tubes being pushed down my throat, and that's when I black out, hoping oblivion has finally agreed to take me.

I wake up and have no goddamned clue where I am. The lights are too bright, the walls were obviously once painted white, but time and dirt have turned them dingy and sallow looking. I try to sit up and realise that I am strapped to a stretcher. A slow moan comes out of my throat when it dawns on me that I am not dreaming. Things start to flash back to me, the phone call with Donnie and then my mother, the pills, the knife, the bath, the ambulance ride.

I notice a fat, middle-aged man dressed in a black uniform. He's not paying attention to me, though it's my guess that he's supposed to. I twist my arms, even though the leather straps dig into my cuts and reopen them, until I get a hand free. I am beyond feeling pain now. I undo the buckles quietly, slowly. He's chattering away with some pretty female nurse who couldn't care less about him but is trying not to be rude and tell him straight out to piss off.

I am in the emergency room of a hospital and look for signs to the waiting room. My feet hit the floor, and Jesus, could it have *been* any colder in there? It's the dead of winter and it doesn't feel like the heat is on in this dirty, overcrowded hospital building.

I make my way to the entrance of the waiting room. I look through the bulletproof glass in the door and see my mother. I try to open it, but the door is locked. She is crying and hunched over, my stepfather is holding her as her body is wracked with sobs. I put my bloody and bandaged hand on the glass. She looks up and sees me and runs to the glass, slipping from my step-father's embrace. About this time I hear the fat security guard asking people 'Where is that girl who was just in this bed?' and I figure I have about five seconds when I hear the footsteps coming behind me. I do not look behind me, I know what is coming and I just want to be near my mom, even if she hates me after what I've done tonight. I start to cry when she starts to cry and she puts her hand to the glass too.

She says one word in the form of a question, and if I could have felt anything at that moment, it would have broken my heart. 'Why?' I cannot hear her, maybe I didn't want to or maybe it was the bulletproof glass and the locked door, and all I can say is that I'm sorry before security guards drag me away.

I am held down by a combination of nurses and security guards and strapped down to this bed again, in this alien room, cold and praying that this is all some horrible nightmare, just like the rest of my life has been.

A nurse comes and sticks a needle hard into my damaged arms. I remember thinking to myself 'She didn't have to be so damned rough. I mean shit, obviously I am *not* having a good day...', but the thought disappears. I am fading into black, and the last thought in my head before the dark claims me are the words 'Can you feel, now?'

CHAPTER 2
A rude awakening

Cold, sharp metal pierces my skin again and I wake up. Sort of. Whatever the nurses gave me has put me into a complacent haze and my limbs move wherever they decide to push them into place. Which happens to be in front of me, as more cold metal touches my body. This time, it's handcuffs. I look down in an amazed stupor and then look up again. The police are arresting me for trying to kill myself? How screwed up is this?

But they aren't arresting me; they are transporting me to a mental hospital. I am placed in the back of a police van and I slip back into sleep until the door is slammed open and I am ordered out of the van.

I am escorted into the county mental hospital. I am guessing it's around 3 am. Red night-lights illuminate the hallways and I cannot help but think that some extremely screwed up individual planned that. Wails of inmates, prisoners, patients – whatever the insane are called in a place like this – greet me and chills go up my spine. I am half convinced that I am actually dead and I am in the waiting room of hell.

The policeman handcuffs me to a cold fake leather bench while he goes to talk to the night orderly. I can hear them arguing. I can hear a female voice telling him 'there just simply isn't any room, you know how busy it gets in here around Christmas time...' and I silently say a prayer of gratitude. The nurse brings me a blanket and I curl up as best as I can on this cold bench, that one wrist is still handcuffed to. I fall asleep.

'Emma... wake up Emma...' my mother's voice whispers to me. I jerk awake and look around. She is not there, just some strange nurse and the policeman from before. 'Wake up Emma. We're moving you.'

Once again, I am loaded into the police van and I am checked into a new hospital, where I am handed a blanket, a pillow and a sheet and shown into a room with two beds. 'Keep quiet, you have a roommate; don't wake her.'

Great.

I am convinced that my roommate is the type of inmate that eats flies and spiders while thinking that she's Santa Claus. I am mildly concerned that there is going to be some horrible incident in the middle of the night with her. Sleep claims me quickly though, and she doesn't bother me.

I am woken up again, after what feels like just a few minutes, by more needles in my arm. I don't even care at this point. I cannot feel the cold any more or the pain in my arms and the ache in my heart. I fall back asleep.

Nurses pound on the door, announcing their unwanted and uncaring presence before entering. I am given a pair of pyjama-style pants, a hospital gown, and a pair of socks. I am told to shower, where I am watched by a nurse who is there to make sure I somehow don't injure myself bathing.

This creeps me out, and I am irritated as the water doesn't seem to get above 78 degrees. Shivering, I put on the crappy, ill-fitting, nearly paper-thin hospital clothes that hang off my broken and emaciated body. The nurse leaves.

I sit on the edge of my bed and notice, now that it is daylight, that there are old bloodstains on it. But I am too exhausted to be as grossed out as I should be. I notice my roommate and she is younger than I am, cute and bouncy and chipper. This annoys the shit out of me. Who the hell is happy in a place like this?

Her name is Cindy, and I don't get to find out why she is here before we are told to go to the dining room for breakfast.

I follow everyone else, seeing as how I don't know where I am going. I look around at the other patients here and I notice that they're all minors. Some of them are zombies, shuffling towards breakfast. I try not to dwell on this thought too long because if I do, fear will kick in that 'they' will turn me into one of those drooling, shuffling patients.

We are served cold, nearly inedible cafeteria food with plastic spoons that are counted up at the end of the meal. I am not hungry and let the other inmates pick from my tray.

Next, we're all herded into a room with half-inch thick windows, scuffs and stains on the cheap linoleum floor, and couches that were most likely brand new about twenty years ago. A doctor comes into the room and all the giggling and talking comes to a stop.

Dr X is a fairly young and not unpleasant looking brown-haired, blue-eyed male doctor, wearing glasses and a white coat. 'Good morning everyone. Please get out your journals.'

The Finer Points of Becoming...

I don't have a journal and somehow, I feel instantly ashamed.

He looks at me and says, 'Emma, I understand you got here late last night. We will provide one for you during this session. You are expected to write in it at the appropriate times. Failure to do so will result in loss of privileges.' I don't say anything at all, I just simply stare and finally nod my head when I feel the rest of the room staring at me.

Dr X continues with the bored monotone of someone who does this every single day. 'Since we have someone new here, let's all introduce ourselves and say why we're here.'

Oh Lord. I roll my eyes as I get flashes of an Alcoholics Anonymous meeting. Everyone goes in turn, announcing their name and why they're here. Some of the patients are so out of it they have no idea what the hell their names are, and say them slowly; like it's a new word they're trying out, off the cover of their journal.

When it is my turn, I stand up and I say 'Hi. My name is Emma. I'm an alcoholic.' Nobody gets the joke, or if they do they don't appreciate it.

Dr X scolds me and says, 'I don't find that very appropriate Emma.'

Chastised, I blush and manage to stammer out 'Uh, I tried to kill myself.' The words sound strange to me, and again I am awash in the feeling that this can't really be happening.

During this group therapy session, people talk about their feelings. I scoff, and sit there silently judging them. Some of them have no reason to be here from what I can tell, other than that they wanted attention. I hate them. They make me sick. I feel superior to them in my pain, in my suffering. My walls go up. 'You will not reach me,' I scrawl on the inside cover of the journal that was passed to me.

I have a private meeting with Dr X right after therapy where he asks me a series of what I imagine to be typical questions for this type of in-patient setting. I lie to nearly all of them and answer flawlessly until he comes to one question that throws me for a loop. 'Are you now, or have you ever been, beaten or been witness to a parent or guardian being beaten?' I pause. I want to say yes, some small part of me wants to say yes and wants help, but I push that weak voice back down and I say 'No' instead. Dr X notices the pause and he looks at me hard. 'Are you sure?' I cross my arms and repeat my answer.

Dr X looks at me until I feel like he can see through me. I fidget. Finally, he breaks the silence and says 'You are here for a mandatory three days Emma. You can use this time to begin to deal with whatever drove you to try to kill yourself, or not. At the end of three days, however, if I decide you aren't making enough progress, I can keep you here as long as I see fit. Do you understand?'

I swallow hard. My tongue feels like it's made of wood, and it refuses to move at all.

I simply nod at him. 'I read the reports of the police and the emergency medical team. I am prescribing some medications that I think will help you. You may go now.'

I pick up the stupid journal and I leave the room. I am ushered back into the group area, where the group has 'free time'. Some pretty Asian girl comes up to me and grabs my arm. 'Did you do this to yourself?'

'Uh, yeah.' I stammer. This idiot acts like I just told her that I was a movie star and gets all kind of excited and gushy on me.

'Oh my God, I wish I could do that to myself! How does it feel?'

I jerk my arm away from her as she's trying to stick her wretched fingers into the rips of skin. I am at a loss for words. I hate her. She is a vile creature and I wish she would just disappear. She does not notice my contempt of her and continues.

'This is my seventh suicide attempt. I swallowed a bottle of aspirin.'

Without any further comment, I walk away. Unlike her, I am not proud of these cuts on my arm, not proud of the fact that I am in here. I sit in a chair as far away from her as possible and begin to brood.

A dorky, tall, white, pimply-faced boy introduces himself as 'Ricky' to me. He begins to explain how this place works; what we are allowed to do and when we're supposed to do it.

When the nurses come in with trays of pills and water, we line up and take whatever is in the cup. I have a little blue pill and a slightly larger white pill in my paper cup.

'What is this?' I ask the nurse.

She curtly responds to me. 'Your medicine.'

'Yeah, I got that. What kind?'

This stocky, ruddy, un-pretty middle-aged nurse who is giving the opiates to the masses looks up at me. Like I am deaf or stupid, she repeats herself. 'YOUR MEDICINE.'

Ricky is behind me and whispers to me quickly. 'Just take it, or she'll call a code on you, and you don't want that.'

I take his advice, and swallow the medication with the tepid cup of what tastes like toilet water. I stick my tongue out and they check to make sure I took them.

An orderly comes in and unlocks a big plastic bin and passes out colouring books and crayons. I scoff. I colour the angel picture they gave me to colour in with the darkest crayons in the box. I colour her wings black. Then I draw blood dripping down them, just to upset people. 'How the HELL is this supposed to make me better?' I think to myself.

A bell rings and we put the books and crayons away. We go to lunch. We are supposed to write in our journals before evening therapy but I don't do it. I think it's stupid. Not as stupid as the crappy colouring books and the cheap, shitty crayons they gave us to colour the pictures with, but still completely retarded and pointless. Besides, where would I even begin?

CHAPTER 3
My first journal

December ??

I know it's December, but I don't know what day it is. How can I know when there are no calendars around the place? Perhaps they think that if we never know what the date is we won't excite ourselves by looking forward to things like birthdays or holidays. This place is stupid and lame. I really don't know how this godforsaken journal is supposed to do anything, and I really don't know what the hell you expect me to write. Your food sucks ass, it's too damned cold in here, and it would be nice if I had a mattress that wasn't blood-covered. Also, perhaps you're not aware of this, but these clothes don't fit me and it would be nice if I had some that did. All in all, I'm having a miserable time. Screw you.

Dr X looks at me with a frozen stare that leaves me genuinely afraid. There is an uncomfortable silence. I wish he'd just yell at me or something, not just stare at me. The haughty demeanour I walked in with fades under his icy gaze.

'Perhaps you didn't understand the directions Emma.' I pick at nothing on my pants.

'You said to write about my feelings. So that's what I did.'

'The directions were to write about your feelings, yes. These are complaints. Secondly, you are supposed to write at least a page a day, half a page in the morning and the evening at the minimum.'

Dr X drops the journal on the desk in front of him and distastefully pushes it back towards me. 'You're not trying Emma. I suggest you start.'

His words thinly conceal an open-ended threat that I might find myself having to stay in this shit hole. I pick up the journal and leave. I go and sit back in the main room and listen to all the other patients talk about nothing important at all. I am growing more and more irritated. I've focused in on the sound and it grows louder in my head, like the buzzing of bees.

I am afraid I'm going to do something horrible, I can see myself screaming at all of them about their stupid, meaningless lives and I feel like I can't breathe. I'm gasping for air when finally group therapy is called and everyone shuts the hell up. The buzzing stops. I can breathe again.

I cross my arms and scowl at every single person while they talk. I make goals for myself in here to keep myself entertained. Today I have decided to practise staring at people until they feel uncomfortable.

My game is interrupted by Dr X's voice. 'Is there a problem Emma?'

I flinch at the sound. Everyone stares at me. Now I feel uncomfortable. 'No.'

He waits for a minute and then looks at the pretty Asian girl who accosted me when I first arrived here with her idiocy and her fingers. Apparently 'Lucy' is her name, and she goes back to talking about how she lives a life of luxury and her parents don't pay attention to her, or something else retarded like that. Everyone nods and mutters words of encouragement. I roll my eyes.

It finally gets to be my turn to talk. 'I don't have anything to say,' I state flatly.

Everyone stares at me again. I ignore their zombie eyes by concentrating on my fingernails. Dr X is staring at me too; I know it. I am frustrated. I really *don't* know what to say.

Dr X speaks. 'OK Emma, let's talk about anything you want. Anything at all.'

I start to cry, I am so damned frustrated, and my showing of emotion upsets me more. I bite the inside of my mouth until I taste blood.

'I don't know what to say. I really don't. I'm frustrated because I don't know what to say.'

As if God somehow hears my thoughts, a bell sounds and Dr X sighs. Therapy is over. I say a silent prayer of gratitude.

Pills. Food. Colouring. I am irritated, and it's swelling inside my chest and I can't control it. The same rotten nurse who spoke to me like I was an idiot when I asked her what medication she was giving me, curtly tells me to clean up the crayons as I am putting them away in the plastic baby wipe box they are contained in.

'I *am* putting them away.' I respond angrily to her demand.

'*What* was that?' she snaps at me.

I don't back down, not to this wretched, hateful woman. 'I SAID, I AM PUTTING THEM AWAY.' I cross my arms.

'Put the damned crayons away, you psycho little bitch.'

I lose it. I pick up the fake plastic Christmas tree that has long since seen better days and throw it at her. 'Shove it!' I yell.

Her face turns beet red and the room goes silent. She walks out of the door quickly and about three seconds later I hear a code being called.

'God *damn* it' I say and drop the box of crayons on the table when I see four male orderlies who look like they double as linebackers for a football team head towards me. I put my hands up slightly and out to my sides as the nurse stands behind them, smirking.

They grab my arms and legs even though I am not resisting and they carry me towards a room. I remember Ricky once telling me that this is the isolation room. This idea does not appeal to me and I begin trying to wiggle my way out of these ungentle hands that are holding me. It's no use though, and I am put face down on this table while hands quickly begin to strap me down.

One of the orderlies is trying to rip off the hemp bracelet that I have on my right wrist. It was Donnie's. 'No. NO! I will take it off, don't rip it!'

For some reason he listens and I take it off and hand it to him right before they grab my hands and strap those down too. A shot goes into my ass, and off to dreamland I go.

I am young here; I don't know how old, maybe four. I am in the first house I remember living in, the one that was painted yellow on the outside and I swore there were ghosts in there. I see my father's tan brown recliner facing the old television we used to have, the one that still had knobs on it and rabbit ears. There is a lace tablecloth, yellowed with age on the scuffed dining table. I am in my room that does not have a door, because it got broken by my father's fists during one of my parents' fights. A sheet with faded cartoon characters is nailed to the top of the door jam, but it does not block the sound of my parents fighting. I hear the sharp slap of what I already know is the sound of an open palm striking someone's face; my mother's face, and she wails. I clutch Tabitha, my little blonde cabbage patch doll tightly. I start to cry. Nobody hears me, and I hear glass break. I am afraid.

'Goddamit Teresa...' I hear my father say and then stop. I hear my mother sniffling. 'See what you did?' he yells and I hear him slap her again. 'You woke up Emma!'

My mother comes into the room, her eyes red-rimmed and with darker red spots on her face where my father's hand had struck her. She lays me back down and tells me to hush and go back to sleep.

'Mommy...' I start crying but she slips from my fingers and goes back out into the living room to keep receiving whatever punishment my father had decided she deserved. I huddle under the blanket, clutching Tabitha, and cry.

I open my eyes. They feel like they weigh a thousand pounds each, and it takes me a few tries to get them all the way open.

I am surprised to find that tears have collected in a tiny pool under my face on the plastic table. I am groggy and thirsty. My lips are like sand; they're so dry they've cracked and I lick them in a vain attempt to moisten them, but my tongue is like sandpaper and I give up.

I begin the task of trying to get out of the leather straps on the table. I get my right hand free and about sixty seconds later I have gotten all of my bonds loose. I pick a corner where I can see everything in the room and huddle up in it.

A sob threatens to break out of my chest. 'No, you do not cry, you are metal; machines don't cry,' I chant to myself over and over, rocking back and forth. The sob is still there and it is spilling into my chant and pissing me off so I say the chant louder until I am practically screaming at myself.

A heavy metal clunking sound comes from the door and I look up as it opens. Dr X is in the doorway. He sighs when he sees me. 'How did you get off the table Emma?'

I look at him with hurt in my eyes. I don't answer. I am clutching myself and rocking, staring at him. He walks into the room and an orderly begins to follow him. He turns and stops the orderly and whispers something to him. The orderly looks at me and then steps back outside. I go back to staring at the floor.

Dr X is standing above me. 'What happened, Emma?'

Years of lying, of not telling people anything about my life or what was going on in it kick in, and I refuse to tell him that the nurse egged me on. He squats down in front of me when I don't answer.

'Emma…'

I look up at him and I can't help myself; tears are spilling onto my white cheeks. 'I am a machine. Machines don't cry.'

His brow furrows slightly and he tilts his head. 'You're not a machine Emma. And you're not violent. Angry yes, but you're not violent. What happened?'

I repeat myself as I stare at the floor, rocking back and forth.

He sighs.

'Emma… I have to keep you here longer now. You know that, right?'

I know. But I don't respond. I just keep rocking.

Dr X pulls a tissue out of his pocket and hands it to me. He walks over to the door and talks to the orderly standing guard outside, and a few moments later, he hands me a cup of water.

I guzzle it, my hands shaking and clutching the paper cup.

Dr X goes to the door. 'Take a few minutes and compose yourself Emma. When you're done, you can come out. It's almost dinner time.'

He walks out of the door and I feel sad that he's gone.

I wipe my cheeks and run my fingers through my choppy black hair. I steel myself, everyone is going to look at me like I'm a psycho when I leave this room, but it's better than being in here. I walk past the tear-stained plastic table and ignore it. I squint at the light in the doorway, and I walk through it.

Pills. Food. Colouring. I pick up my journal. I begin to write.

CHAPTER 4

Machine or ghost?

December ??

Oh God just look at me now... one night opens words and utters pain... I cannot begin to explain to you... this... I am not here. This is not happening. Oh wait, it is isn't it?

You've forced my hand to paper, and now the words don't come, a million things are locked inside my goddamned head. And I still can't breathe, long after you've taken me out of the straps... should I count my words here? Do I need to have it exactly one page or is it OK if it's a few words less?

You want to know how I feel? I feel dead and hollow and I wish I hadn't called the paramedics. That's how I feel. Ghost.

I am a ghost. I am not here, not really. You see skin and cuts and frailty... these are symptoms, you know, of a ghost. An unclear image with unclear thoughts whispering vague things...

If I told you what was really in my head, you'd never let me leave this place. And I have no desire to spend time in hell while I'm still, in theory, alive.

I bite the insides of my cheek until I taste blood as Dr X reads my evening journal entry.

This is what being honest feels like... goes through my head. I wait for him to finish reading.

That's it, he's going to label you crazy and you're never getting out of here, I tell myself silently and sigh. I don't care right now though; either I'm so damned raw that I have gone numb, or I'm still sedated, or maybe it's both. I just simply don't care.

Dr X looks up at me and I am startled by the expression on his face. He's not angry with me. In fact, he almost looks sad.

So the bastard does *feel something,* I tell myself again.

He looks down once more, at tear and blood stained admissions of being completely lost, hidden within sentences that don't quite make sense. We lock eyes. For once, for the first time, I am not the first one to drop my gaze. He does.

'No, Emma. You don't have to write exactly a full page any more,' he says softly. 'You may go now.'

I freeze. Normally I bolt out of this session, which feels like a trial without a jury where I've already been declared guilty. But I feel nothing. He says nothing.

I move in near slow motion, expecting this to be some sort of trick. Like he's going to reveal himself to be the unfeeling sadist that I have been imagining he really is; laughing at me while condemning me to a life sentence in this place. Condemning me to being a zombie.

Dr X notices my hesitation. 'I'm not going to punish you, Emma.'

I am confused and just a little bit uncomfortable, but I take his words at face value and leave anyway.

Ricky is outside talking to Lucy. I silently wish her a more successful suicide attempt and walk on by. Ricky quickly ends his conversation with Lucy and comes to sit next to the chair furthest from everyone else in the room, which is where I've made my home.

'Hi Emma,' he says. It takes me a minute to look up at him. They've prescribed me about three more medications since *The Incident* and my brain feels like it consists of nothing but fog any more. I look up at him blankly.

'The meds are hitting ya pretty hard aren't they? What are they giving you?' he asks me.

I try to think. I can't remember the long foreign machine names of all the *dones* and *zones* and *iums* they've prescribed me.

'I... uh... don't know.'

My mouth is unbearably dry. I feel like I've sunk into this chair though, and I can't move. My stitches itch in my arms. I look down and realise that half the cuts don't have stitches, and the thought mildly creeps me out before I look back up at Ricky.

'Well...' he looks around to make sure nobody is close by before he continues. 'There is kind of a *black market* around here so to speak, and whatever you're on must be good. So if you can find a way not to swallow it, ya know, you could probably trade it for other stuff if you wanted to.'

'People want to buy something I've had to hide *in my mouth* for at least two minutes and then let dry out before I *sell* it to them?' I ask incredulously.

'Yeah. Like Lucy over there, *major* pill head. And I don't know if you've met Frank yet, the little quiet skinny black kid. Him too.'

I stare at Ricky, inadvertently making him feel uncomfortable. My eyes have become razorblades without me even knowing it.

'Hey, Emma, look, I'm just trying to help OK?' he offers. 'I mean, you haven't really gone out of your way to make friends around here, and I just figured, ya know, you might want to know stuff around here. Stuff that the staff don't tell you.'

I soften a bit at his awkward demeanour and his attempts to help me. I've been nothing but rude to everyone, he's right. Maybe I misjudged him by lumping him into the same category as the worthless zombies that roam the halls.

'Thank you Ricky. I'll just... uh... keep that in mind.'

Ricky visibly relaxes. He smiles an awkward, unsure, too-kind smile.

I look down at the doodles in my journal. I want to be alone. He doesn't pick up on this. Or maybe he does and ignores it, refusing to let me be alone for whatever reason.

'I just... ya know... want you to know you have someone to talk to that isn't a *narc* or a doctor, Emma. I feel kind of bad for you...' he looks down and fidgets with his hands before he continues.

'...you're obviously hurting. Not like some of the *other* people in here,' he says and looks distastefully at Lucy.

I smile. He smiles. I actually start to laugh at our mutual hatred of the *poseur* Lucy. Our short-lived laughter dies down. Silence.

'What put you in here Ricky?' I ask him, my voice as soft as falling snow. I am again reminded that I am a ghost. I don't seem to talk very loud any more.

He looks down and sighs before starting. I wait with the patience of Buddha.

'My dad was a real jerk. Ya know, he hit my mom all the time. Then, when she finally left, he started hitting *me*. And I wasn't big enough to fight him off, so it just kept going on ya know? One day I'll be big enough.'

He nods, more to himself than to me, assuring himself that one day it will stop. I feel sick.

'So, I tried to kill myself. I uh, tried to hang myself but my dad walked in. And uh, now I'm in here.'

I notice faint scars that crisscross his face, amongst the pockmarks from the bad acne. I don't know why, but I put my hand on his. He grasps my tiny white hand tightly in his big ruddy one. We look at each other and say nothing. I feel uncomfortable with human touch though, and I let go.

'Me too,' I whisper. The words start to come as if I'm possessed.

'My parents fought all the time until the divorce. They dragged that out for years. *Years.* Can you imagine that? Telling your kids over and over you're getting a divorce and then not? It was pretty screwed up.'

I'm looking down at my fingers, not at him. But I find myself wanting to say more.

'Except my dad didn't just hit her, it was *all* of us. I used to be daddy's little girl. Then I started to look like my mom when I started to grow up and it seemed, after that, that he hated me. He wouldn't hug me any more. In fact, I remember trying to hug him once in a restaurant and him pushing me off in embarrassment, telling me that *People are going to think something is wrong.*'

I shudder briefly at this memory, but I continue to describe it.

'When I looked at him in shock, that was the beginning of the end with us. Like

I said, things had been bad with him and mom for years.'

I pause. I lick my lips, trying to get some damned moisture on them since they won't give us *ChapStick* here. I am on autopilot, talking and not really talking; some part of my mind is still not here, not associating these words with real events, with real people. I sigh, a sigh of exhaustion; it's all I can do to get enough air to continue to whisper.

'I used to pray you know, pray to God that He would somehow stop it. All the nights of listening to my mother scream and things breaking. Of holding my brother and sister and listening to them cry and begging me to stop it.'

My voice is slow and steady like a freight train at night.

'I was too young, and we were always told that they'd put us in foster homes where people would rape us if we ever said anything. So we explained away the bruises, and my mom wore big sunglasses whenever she left the house. And we invented car accidents if the bruising was too bad to cover with make-up.'

Ricky just listens. He isn't shocked. He isn't surprised. He listens to me because he knows. He knows the shame and the guilt and the sorrow and the rage. And he does not judge me. He just listens.

'I know his childhood was bad, my father's. I mean, he has said bits and pieces... his father left him and like, two of his siblings died... and the man his mother remarried was an abusive prick.'

I've always tried to justify my father. Because when he wasn't angry and hurting us, he was the most wonderful man in the world to me. He was strong and handsome with beautiful blue eyes and an easy laugh. I smile a little as I bring to mind a good memory of my father, and feel it's not fair if I don't tell it. I've told bad stories, and now I feel like I have to defend him. Ricky waits for me to finish or continue. Just waits. He isn't impatient at my pauses, or horrified at my story. He just sits and waits and listens. I am comforted by this, and continue.

'I remember one time, he found a little lizard on a glue trap, still alive. He sat at the kitchen table with a jar of flour for five hours, ever so gently prying this creature's tiny little claws and body from the trap before letting him go. He wasn't all bad. But when he *was* bad...'

I trail off and finally stop. I see no reason to keep talking. Ricky waits for a minute and gently touches my hand again, just briefly. He walks away. Moments later he brings me a glass of water, and I am stunned by this act of kindness.

'Thank you, Ricky.'

'You're welcome, Emma.'

He says nothing more.

Suddenly, he's not awkward and he gracefully bows out, leaving me alone to contemplate the past. I look around and notice that the Christmas tree has been taken out of the room. Torn Christmas decorations are still hanging though, faded and God only knows how old.

It's starting to look like I am going to spend my Christmas in this dingy, dirty, tomb.

The nurses come in with trays. It's medication time. One by one, we file in line and we accept whatever is given to us. The snotty, wretched nurse is replaced by a thin, anaemic looking one who is quiet and not completely bitchy. She even smiles at some of the patients that have been here longer, ones she recognises.

I don't fight it any more. I don't have the strength to. I swallow the pills and silently walk back to my seat at the edge of the room to wait for the next wave of comfortable numbness to set in.

My journal sits loosely on my lap. All I can do is stare at the wall.

CHAPTER 5

'A dream is a wish that your heart makes…'

December ??

I'm tired and jittery from all the medication they're giving me. I don't know what the date is any more. I feel sick to my stomach all the time, but they expect me to eat anyway. Have you ever taken this shit they're giving me? Have you? It's like taking a fucking speedball and it's scaring the crap out of me. I'm exhausted but you won't let me sleep, the meds won't let me eat without throwing up for half an hour after dinner, and I'm stuck in my head.

It's late at night and I am writing this by the creeping yellow light coming in through the broken plastic blinds that cover the clouded-with-dirt window. I just kind of scribbled nonsense tonight in my journal so I wouldn't get in trouble for not writing anything. But something is inside me, trying to claw its way out of my chest and onto this paper.

I'm afraid to write though. I know about child protection laws and I'm afraid of my parents. And what happens if I tell the truth and nobody believes me? Then my parents will beat me when I get home for *almost getting them in trouble.*

I close my eyes against an unwelcome thought; my father. *He's angry at me for being awake. He thinks that hitting me will somehow lull me to sleep. I'm crying and he starts screaming at me to shut up and go to sleep.*

I'm what... twelve here? I could never sleep very well. I've always had insomnia. When I was very little, the doctors my parents took me to, after nights of listening to me scream in my sleep, said it was 'Night

Terrors'. They said to let me keep the light on if it helped. They still didn't let me keep the goddamned night-light on though. Bastards.

Anyway, I'm not sure I had 'Night Terrors'. I think I was probably so traumatised from listening to my parents fight all the damned time. I think that it really did a number on my brain, so that even in sleep the fear and the bad thoughts wouldn't go away.

To be quite honest with you, talking to Ricky earlier really kind of messed me up some, and for what reason I'm not sure.

I've heard my friends, other kids, talk about getting knocked around by their parents. Hell, half of my friends had similar situations as mine to endure – parents who should never have got married and sure as hell should never have had us. And who fought all the time, fists and all, leaving us wrecked, sad, depressed, and way too old for how young we are. I'm sixteen and feel ancient. Thoughts and memories race through my brain now, that I don't want to remember. And, since I'm falling apart, my little mantras don't work any more.

Let's say, theoretically, (and the reason I say this is because if it wasn't *theoretical, you could call the police, and then you could take me away from my family, and I wouldn't want that any more than I like being in this hell hole...) that I have a friend. She's grown up in an abusive home. Her earliest memories are of listening to her parents scream and yell at each other. She's watched her father slam her mother's head into a metal filing cabinet at some age too young to recall. She's watched her mom put on layers of make-up until it just looks like she has permanent dark circles under her eyes. You know, like those older ladies you find at the drugstore buying pancake make-up in the attempt to hide those dark circles...*

And she hates herself for it. You see, this girl blames herself for it. Partly because she thinks it wouldn't have happened if she wasn't born. That's what her father says anyway. And partly because she didn't put a stop to it. She never was strong enough or could get out of the house fast enough to stop any of it, and she is so sick with guilt that... let's say that maybe she's even tried to kill herself, that's how sick it makes her. And now she's sitting in some dirty mental hospital, scribbling pathetically in some journal trying to sort out all the mess in her head...

I have to stop writing. I re-read what I've just written, and even though I haven't said my own name and even though I put *theoretically* on paper, I wonder – can they still call the police? Can they still put me in some foster home? And if they did, would it be worse?

I chew on my pencil, deep in thought. I ponder this very seriously, but at a distance, like it's some mathematical puzzle that I need to solve rather than it being, well, you know, my life.

I come to a decision. I nod to myself, thoughtfully. Yes. It *would* be worse to be in a foster home. I mean, my parents are divorced, have been for about a year or however long it's been, right? So what the hell is my problem? Why does this still upset me so much? Shouldn't I feel better now? Shouldn't the sounds of fists meeting flesh have started to fade?

WHAT THE HELL IS WRONG WITH ME? I press so hard with my pencil as I write this that I rip through part of the paper. Great, I think to myself frowning. Even when I am trying to get everything out, something falls apart. Like paper.

I'm having an internal debate about whether I should turn this journal paper in or not when another unpleasant thought assaults me.

I drop the pencil and cover my ears and curl up into a tiny ball to protect myself.

I'm sitting in the living room, watching some stupid cartoon about some girl who has a terrible life with horrible stepsisters and an evil stepmother who make her clean all the time. The mice are singing some song about how a dream is a wish your heart makes, or something like that. And then my parents come home. They're drunk. My mother looks slightly panicky. They hand the babysitter too much money and shoo her out of the door quickly. They immediately go to their bedroom, and the door slams shut.

I hear arguing. I sigh – I think I'm eight or so here. I turn the television up, trying to ignore them. They get louder. I turn the television up some more. This is never going to stop. I remember thinking how I may as well get used to it. I am trying to focus on these little mice and the blonde girl and how she wants to go to a 'ball', whatever that is. I think it's where people dress up and dance funny.

My dad comes out and is too nice, and tells me to go to bed. 'But dad...' I start, and stop just as quickly when his face turns cruel and mean. I can hear my mother crying in the other room as I walk by.

'But I have to say goodnight to Mommy...' I start again.

'She'll come in later and tuck you in. Get your ass in bed. NOW!'

I run off to bed. He shuts the lights out, ALL of them, and closes the door.

The way this house is set up is that my room is adjoining my parents' room. And cheap tract housing doesn't tend to have thick walls, so I end up hearing way more than I ever want to hear from that cursed room.

The sounds are getting louder, the screaming is louder, and Jesus, my mother's screams are always the worst part. It's like hearing a dog being beaten and not being able to do anything but feel sad when you hear the pathetic yelp, and hating the bastard who is doing it.

My mother sounds more terrified than usual. Something, this time, is very, very wrong. I can't remember being more afraid, a vice has gripped me and I can't move, only listen as the sounds grow louder and more grotesque. Things are breaking, and my father is screaming like he is someone else. I hold my little brother and sister as they beg me to do something, to stop it.

'If we pray hard enough God will listen and He'll stop him, and daddy won't kill her.'

I keep trying to sneak out of my window to get help. This one is bad and I am afraid. Really afraid. But the son of a bitch keeps coming and checking on us and I am too terrified to do anything but pretend to sleep. Once he almost catches me, but he is too coked-out to notice that I am in a different bed than before.

I keep at the window, but it is child-proof and I can't get it unlocked. My tiny fingers cannot twist the metal tab hard enough to get the window open. Even if I could, he'd definitely hear me before I made it through to the backyard, over the six-foot tall fence and to the neighbour's house on the other side.

So we pray in vain. We pray and we cry ourselves to sleep to the sounds of things *breaking, our father yelling, our mother's sobbing pleas.*

Next day we wake up and all stand in a line at the door and kiss our father goodbye as he goes to work...

No. No, I'm not going to remember this... *NO NO NO NO NO!* I start saying to myself, softly at first, but growing louder.

My roommate stirs. Oh Jesus, I'm about to get a code called... why won't *this* particular memory go away? Why this one, of *all* of them?

I start repeating. 'No, this isn't happening, this did NOT HAPPEN TO YOU, THIS DID NOT HAPPEN TO YOU...' over and over again.

If I tell myself this enough, it usually goes away. They are mantras that protect me.

I tear up the cursed pieces of paper that I now blame for stirring up these thoughts, rip them into teeny tiny shreds, hoping to rip the thoughts up too. It's not working.

Good goddamned job Emma, you started writing and now look what it did to you, now you're sitting here crying and sobbing all over again, and where have all your tears got you?

'SHUT UP!' I scream at myself. My roommate wakes up.

'EMMA!' she yell-whispers at me, her hair tousled by sleep and her voice low and hoarse. 'Shut the hell up before the nurses wake up or the orderlies in the hall on the rounds hear you. It's late and I'm tired, and to be honest, I really don't care what the hell you're saying! Just shut up and go back to sleep!'

In a final fit of drama, she throws herself back down on the bed and covers her head with her pillow.

I am still curled up in a ball, shreds of paper lying around me. I'm not quiet, like she wants, but at least I'm whispering, and she doesn't say anything else.

I repeat one of my mantras. 'This is not happening. This is not real. This did not happen to you. That was someone else.'

Normally, like I said, this set of phrases I can repeat *ad nauseam* until the thoughts fade back to black, back to the dark part of my brain where I keep these horrors, and I try very, very hard not to think about them.

Tonight this memory is not going away though. Tonight, just like I did those years ago, I end up crying myself to sleep, praying for the thoughts to go away.

CHAPTER 6
Visitors

Sleep didn't claim me until I saw the gentle changing of the night sky to early morning, and only then did the demons of the night release their hold on me as they faded into the night. I closed my eyes, and it seemed like just a few minutes later it was time to wake up.

Exhausted I half-heartedly combed my hair and brushed my teeth. My roommate glared at me, obviously still irritated from the night before. I sighed and wished I could have cared more, but it would have taken energy I simply didn't have.

As I walked down the hallway, I heard

a noise I hadn't heard before and it took me a few steps to realise that I had begun to do what I called the zombie shuffle. Horrified, I made an extra effort to pick my feet up when I walked, and straightened my bony shoulders, determined to cling to whatever shreds of dignity I had left.

When we finally entered the main room, I shuddered. Someone had turned on the heat either too late or not high enough, and it was freezing cold. The cheap slippers did nothing to block the icy chill from the floor, and as I settled into the uncomfortable plastic chair to await the crappy food we were here to eat, I awkwardly picked up my legs and crossed them, balancing precariously on the chair, hoping to warm my feet by tucking them into the crooks of my legs.

Bored and tired orderlies brought the food into the room, long since gone cold and never really edible in the first place. I'm not hungry, but I've learned that if you don't eat, you get in trouble. As I'm already underweight, I have to choke down at least part of the rubber eggs and congealed oatmeal, since I've been threatened with intravenous feedings if I keep skipping meals, and I'd rather choke down a few bites of this crap than to have yet another needle stuck into my painfully sore arms.

I don't remember feeling pain like this in quite some time, and I'm not sure it's quite like anything I've ever felt – the feeling of holes in your veins and so many cuts in your arms they outnumber the skin there. It's a different kind of pain from the type of pain that beatings deliver, and I'm not used to it.

I find myself staring at my arms often; like a train wreck I find it impossible not to stare at the mess that's laid out before me, even though it's sad and tragic and disgusting.

The meds come. The evil nurse is gone, the one from the day before is still here and I am relieved by her semi-friendly presence. When I take the paper cup of water, I am surprised by its coldness. I look up at her and she smiles. She had apparently gone to the effort of filling the water pitcher with filtered, cold tap water. When the cold water hit my dry mouth, I breathed a silent prayer of gratitude. This kindly nurse patted me on the shoulder and I actually smiled at her gratefully, before I walked off and got into my chair for morning group therapy.

I'm having a hard time staying awake during this session. A box of tissue is being passed around like a cookie plate. I pass. I don't have the energy or the tears to cry after last night's painful ordeal of remembering the past.

When it gets to my turn, Dr X looks at me and gives me the 'It's your turn' look. I clear my throat and fidget with my pants, and I begin to talk about my parents' divorce. It's as close to the truth as I can get without revealing too much about what's really going on.

'My parents began their divorce when I was twelve years old,' I begin.

The Finer Points of Becoming...

Dr X interrupts me. 'And how old are you now?' he asks.

'I'm sixteen.' I respond flatly. He looks slightly confused. 'Their divorce lasted... for four years?' Dr X asks me.

'No, for about 3 years.'

Dr X shakes his head slightly. 'Continue, Emma.'

'My parents didn't have a good marriage. They fought all the time. And I mean, really fought. You know, threw things, screaming and yelling all the time.' Ricky nods understanding. I continue.

'Finally, after years of dealing with them fighting, they decided to get a divorce. But you know, every month they'd stop the divorce and try to work things out. A month later they were back to square one, and they'd start the divorce all over again.'

I carefully measure my thoughts, my ⸱⸱. The wrong slip of the tongue could land me in foster care.

'And how did that contribute to your being here today, Emma?' Dr X asks me.

I pause and think of how to answer his question. 'It led me here because... I was depressed about the divorce and their fighting I guess. But I didn't really realise it, you know? I was the oldest child and I was so busy taking care of everyone, my mom, my siblings, that I forgot I had feelings too. And one day I just snapped and couldn't deal with it any more, and that's how I ended up here.'

Dr X nods his approval at my co-operation in this session. I yawn tiredly. I'm so tired my eyes are tearing up, and I wrap my arms around myself to keep warm.

The session ends. We colour. We go to education and I practise math problems that I remember from the fifth grade – or it might have been the year after that, when I was eleven. Whatever... I stare at the sheet of paper for a very long time, not so much because I can't do the problems, but because I'm having a hard time seeing.

The pills have kicked in, and brought with them a wave of almost comfortable numbness, or at least apathy, and that's fine with me at this point. Free time comes and everyone is doing something but me. I'm sitting in my chair, at the end of the room, with my notebook, when a nurse comes in and tells me that I have a visitor.

I blink. 'Who is it?' I ask, a sinking feeling in my stomach.

'Your mother,' she replies.

I am torn between excitement and self-disgust. I am escorted into the visiting area, and I sit nervously while I wait for my mom to enter.

The door opens. My mother walks in, shoulders back, make-up obviously just redone to hide the fact that she was crying. Maybe nobody else knows or notices, but I know. I've seen her cry my whole life, and I know how she looks when she tries to hide it.

My mom and I stand there, face to face. Finally, we hug. She hugs me tightly, forgetting her composure, and her touch feels protective and warm at first, and then it's like she switches off, and then I'm hugging a statue. Awkwardly, we let go of each other and when I look at her face, she has the mask back on, and then she's not really my mom any more, not the mom I know, soft and loving and pretty.

We sit down. Small talk ensues. How are you doing in here? Are they treating you well? How is the food? How are your arms doing? Is the doctor nice? And then, the question that I was half expecting but still wasn't prepared for.

'What are you talking to them about Emma?' I stare at my pyjamas under my mom's scrutiny. 'Uh, nothing really. Just ya know, how I'm feeling, and how the medications are, and stuff like that.'

She nods, not really believing me. 'I heard you attacked a nurse Emmy. Why did you do that?' she asks sadly.

I can't tell her. I don't know why. Maybe I'm afraid she won't believe me, but I don't say a word.

My mom is fidgeting with her bag and finally gets so frustrated she explodes. 'What is WRONG with you Emma? You were supposed to get better when I got away from your father. And now this? You're COMPLETELY embarrassing us Emma. Do you know how that feels? How that makes me look?'

I grit my teeth and, for once, I stand up for myself.

'No Mom, I don't know how that makes you feel. And for once, I don't give a shit.'

My mother gasps at my language. I've never talked to her like this. On cue, she starts to cry.

'Oh *stop* it already.' I continue. 'It was always about you, and always about dad. It was never about us, about us kids. We couldn't feel anything, we couldn't have friends, we had to be your perfect little children to show off to your friends and now, *now*, you find out that things weren't so perfect, but you refuse to take ANY blame for it.'

My mother starts to cry. 'Oh, my God, you hate me, I'm such a bad mother...' she starts before I interrupt.

'STOP IT! Not *everything* is about you, OK? This is about me. *This is about me*, do you understand? I couldn't be everything you wanted. You wanted to pretend that Dad never happened, that the years of fighting and all the horrible things we saw and heard and covered up because you *asked* us to, never happened. And maybe *you* were able to, but I wasn't. And neither were my Paul or Rosemary. And I tell you what, you'd better watch *them* close, or they'll end up in here just like me.'

My mother stares at her purse, clutched tightly in her lap. My words have struck her to the core and she can't even look at me right now. Finally, she remembers she has a voice.

'Is that really why you're in here Emma? I thought it was because your boyfriend...'

I see the pain in her face and I can't help but feel like an asshole for what I've just said. But I can't lie any more either.

'Mommy, it wasn't him. It's everything. It's everything I saw and everything I hid and the fact that when you got remarried, you forgot about me. I was your little helper, but not your daughter. It's about losing my brother. It's about things I can't tell you in here right now, but if it makes you feel better, you can blame it on my boyfriend.'

My mom looks at me and calmly says, 'I've called your father.'

My blood runs cold. 'Why... would you do that?'

'Because you're his daughter, and I think that he should know what happened. He says he's got some appointments and trips he needs to cancel, but he's worried about you and wants to come and see you.'

I never really thought about punching my mother before, but the thought crosses my mind. I grit my teeth and cross my arms.

'You don't want to see him?' my mom asks me, surprised.

I stare at her as if she just told me that she's convinced the earth is flat. 'Mom, what do you think? I mean, really? With everything that's happened, what do you think?'

She stammers. 'I just thought, you could... you know, use your family right now.'

I'm furious. I don't remember being this mad at her, this frail, beautiful, fragile, kind human being before. But now, I want to choke her.

'MOM. I... really... REALLY... wish you hadn't done that.'

'But why?' she asks me, like she's confused.

I stare straight into her beautiful hazel eyes and steel myself.

'Because, mother... because of big sunglasses and lying to schoolteachers and inventing car accidents to cover up your black eyes and broken ribs. Because we sat there and starved when *he* wouldn't pay child support. Because I sat at the goddamned door with a baseball bat and a telephone in case his threats against you rang true and he did come to do what he threatened to do. *That's* why.'

My mother's mouth drops. 'Emmy... don't say those things Emmy. Remember, we don't talk about those things.'

'Yes Mom. I remember. That's why I'm in here, looking like this.'

An orderly knocks on the door and announces that visiting time is over.

My mother and I look at each other awkwardly, and hug.

'I love you,' she says.

'I love you too, Mom.'

'You aren't telling them too much are you?' she asks, afraid.

I sigh. 'No Mommy, I'm not.'

She's visibly relieved. She leaves the room.

The orderly comes and escorts me back into the main room.

I just sit and laugh to myself.

CHAPTER 7

Dinner

I walk around for the rest of the day in a coma. My head is spinning from lack of sleep, pills, and the visit with my mother. Is it really possible that she has no damned clue why I am in here? Did she really think that the memories would just go away when the ink dried on the divorce papers? Was I too hard on her?

I remember her eyes, and how many times they'd cried, and I think that maybe I was. I am stricken with guilt and catch myself on the verge of tears all day. *I am a bad daughter*, I tell myself. Is it so wrong to want someone to understand what the hell I'm going through though?

'EMMA!' I snap out of my thoughts to the unpleasant sound of someone yelling at me. I look and realise that it's dinner time and I'm still slumped in my chair, not at the table like I am supposed to be.

I'm a child again, hearing my father's voice yell at me to come for dinner. Mom runs into my bedroom wide-eyed and grabs my arm, practically dragging me out of my room and out of my little fantasy world of dolls and houses, to sit at the dinner table and listen to them fight some more.

'Emmy, what's wrong with you?' my mother asks me. 'Didn't you hear me? Now you've upset your father...'

And the familiar feeling of knots return to my stomach as we walk down the hallway to the dining room.

My father's steel-grey eyes, eyes that match mine, shoot razors at me from his seat at the head of the table. I start to shake. My mother sits me down at the table, at my father's left side. I attempt a smile, a shy, unsure, crooked hint of a smile, and I say 'Hi Daddy.' No smile meets mine, just eyes that cut through me and leave me feeling smaller than I am.

'EMMA!' I hear the voice again and realise that I have been standing, paralysed, in the middle of the room. Everyone turns to stare at me. Just like my mother had done, a nurse comes and grabs me by the arm and half drags me to sit at a table for a dinner that I don't want to eat. She sits me down next to Ricky, who moves his chair over to make room for me.

I feel everyone staring at me and unconsciously smile the same shy, awkward, hint of a grin I did that day back at the dinner table. My eyes blur when I see nobody smiling back at me and I am ashamed of myself for being so afraid of them that I am ready to cry.

I clear my throat and I stare at the tray intently. I think it's meatloaf. I make a face when I notice the unnatural ketchup-red colour that it is on top, and the burnt, crusty black it is on one side. I pick at the meal with my spoon, the only utensil I've been allowed to eat with since I threw the Christmas tree at the nurse.

After what seems like forever at this uncomfortable table, I pick up my tray and go to place it back in the steel carts they came in. The same nurse who dragged me to my seat eyes the barely touched food and looks at me. 'Sit back down and finish eating.'

'Sit down and finish eating, Emma. That's good food you're letting go to waste,' my father tells me as he eats another forkful of his own. I freeze and stare at my plate in a panic. I can't finish eating this plate of food, it's too much and I'm so afraid of being here that I can hardly swallow for the lump in my throat that threatens to break into a sob.

I stare down at my tray and tell myself that just a few more bites will do it, just do what they say so you don't get into any more trouble. I sit back down. Ricky looks at me. He leans over and whispers, 'You OK, Emmy?'

Paul's fork freezes in mid-air and he kicks me under the table to get my attention. 'You OK, Emmy?'

My father stares at my mother, as if this is somehow her fault.

The colour drains from her face and she forces a smile. 'Emmy, finish your dinner,' she says, trying to be gentle, her voice starting to crack.

I'm aware that something bad is going to happen to her if I don't finish eating this mound of food on my plate. I begin to take bites, tiny bites of food as my family stares at me. Time seems to stand still as I scoop up the food, put it into my mouth and swallow.

Ricky nudges me in the ribs. 'Emma...' he starts and I am again here in the hospital. I begin to take bites of food once again. The same knots are in my stomach, and I feel like throwing up.

'What the hell is wrong with her, Teresa?' my father snaps at my mother. My father turns to nobody and starts yelling, 'I work twelve hours a day to make sure we have food on the table and you ungrateful brats won't even eat it! Well fine, nobody is leaving the table until Emma is done with dinner.' My father crosses his arms and stares at me. They all stare at me, the rest of them pleadingly.

My mother is trying not to cry. 'Emmy, you're being selfish...' and my father grabs the fork out of my hand, scoops too much food on it for a little girl and forces it into my hand. My cheeks burn red and I give up. I start shovelling food into my mouth, barely chewing now, just to get it down.

I stare at a smudge on the wall across the room, and begin to shovel food into my mouth until I can't eat any more, until I'm sure I'll throw up if I take one more bite. I blindly stand up, choking on the world's shittiest meatloaf and a head of bad memories and put the tray back into the metal thing. The nurse nods her approval and I think to myself that *she* could probably stand to eat *less* dinner. I sit down for a few minutes before I realise that dinner is going to come back up.

After I've finally finished eating, and the kitchen is cleaned up, my parents begin to argue about something miniscule, something I don't remember, and I feel bile burn the back of my throat.

I run into the bathroom and don't quite make it before the vomit begins to pour out of my stomach, my hand clamped over my mouth to keep it in so I can get the bathroom door shut and nobody will hear me.

I throw up dinner, every last bit of it. My body heaves, over and over again, to get that poisoned dinner out of me, and tears run down the side of my face...

I stand up very fast and begin to walk quickly to my room. When I hit the end of the hallway, I burst into a dead sprint and make it into my room in just enough time to feel the dinner coming up.

I hit my knees too hard on the bathroom floor and throw up hard in the toilet. Tears run down my face and blur my eyes.

I throw up until there is nothing left. I feel only slightly better, and I rinse out my mouth and take a swig of the neon-green mint mouthwash that burns my mouth every time I use it. I splash water on my face and sneak out of the bathroom quietly.

Shaking from the effort, I am finally done throwing up and I flush the toilet and quickly rinse my mouth out. I brush my teeth in record time and walk back into the main room.

I breathe a sigh of relief when I realise that everyone is engrossed in a movie that has apparently just been put on, and that my absence has gone unnoticed. I sneak into a chair and a few minutes later some kid I don't know the name of hands me a folded slip of paper. I stare at it, puzzled, when the kid sighs and shoves it into my hand.

I unfold the tiny piece of paper and peer at it intently in the dim glow of the television set, to read the scrawled words.

I sigh. Well, my absence had *almost* gone unnoticed. Ricky had noticed, and had written me a note. *Are you OK? – Ricky* is all it says.

Are you OK? I read the words at least ten times before they sink into my brain. I stifle a laugh that I know will turn into a hysterical crying fest should it crack my lips.

A crayon is passed back to me covertly. I hold the green stub in my hand and look around to make sure nobody sees me writing. I write my response and refold the paper. I bother the kid in front of me again and whisper to him to pass the note and crayon stub back to Ricky.

I roll my eyes at the movie choice. It's some stupid Christmas movie about a kid who wants a bow and arrow set for Christmas, or something like that. I feel staring eyes, and

I look up. It's Ricky. He frowns at me as he shrugs and lifts his hands up slightly in a *what the hell?* kind of gesture.

I had been too tired and my head too full to deal with his well-meaning but unwanted question, and I had written a single word in reply — *yes*. Obviously he doesn't believe me.

I ignore him and focus on the movie, half asleep, half awake, lulled to a not-quite-awake state by the dim lights and the fact the heater has finally kicked in after a whole day of having my ass frozen off.

I focus in on the sound of the television and drift off, my mind imagining some other family, some other Christmas I did not experience. I hear everyone laugh through my haze. I chuckle with them softly, though I don't really hear what they're laughing at. It is a nice feeling to laugh at something, even if it isn't real.

I hear whispering become a dull roar and a nurse comes in and yells at everyone to be quiet or she'll turn the movie off. Everyone quietens down, and again I am left alone to dream of cookies and trees and presents wrapped under the tree, and – most importantly – nobody fighting.

I let the feeling enfold me, and picture my family at Christmas, Paul and Rosemary and Mom and my father all laughing and giving each other presents like the family on television. I remember my dogs, the ones that Rosemary and I had to leave behind when we moved into the only apartment my mother could afford after the divorce, running through the house excitedly amongst the friendly commotion.

I swear I can smell gingerbread when the lights are turned back on.

'Awww...' everyone complains in unison. My eyes strain to open and I begin to breathe too fast when I realise where I am. I am not part of the quaint family movie we'd just been watching after all.

Everyone begins packing up the main room as the nurse rewinds the movie on the tired VCR player. Everything in this damned place is tired and broken. I am no exception.

As I shuffle off to my room, my roommate bouncing annoyingly cheerfully ahead of me, I am tired and disappointed with myself for getting lost in some picture-perfect fantasy of a happy family.

It's not that I don't love my step-dad, and it isn't that I'm not glad as hell that my parents have finally divorced and I don't have to watch their hellish fights any more. No, I just wish that it had never been that way at all; that my life wasn't so miserable that I had to pretend that I was someone and somewhere else to feel comforted.

I don't even feel the cold water on my face as I get ready for bed. I am still thinking of my mother and feeling torn about our meeting today, part of me feeling guilty and part of me feeling justified in standing up for myself the way I did.

The Finer Points of Becoming...

'Lights out!' I hear someone say, and wearily I walk to my bed. By the time my head hits the pillow, I have already fallen asleep.

CHAPTER 8
Interlude

I open my eyes to the smell of homemade cinnamon buns and hot coffee wafting through the house. I'm warm, snuggled in my quilt, next to Paul and Rosemary, who aren't awake yet, but will be as soon as they feel me stir next to them. I try to stay very still and enjoy the quiet. I look at the window and it's frosted over on the outside, but the coming sun has started to melt it and tiny drops of water run and crisscross the frost, erasing it. Everything is calm and beautiful.

We're all asleep in our new pyjamas, a tradition that happens every Christmas Eve so we'll look nice in the pictures my parents take, pictures that when they get developed three months later, will be critiqued and criticised. Only the best ones will make it into the photo album. I don't like pictures, and they make me nervous. I never seem to look quite right in pictures, always like a deer in headlights or not smiling right.

My thoughts are interrupted by noise. I hear my parents talking. I frown and try to make out what they're saying. Paul stirs next to me. Rosemary has the unfortunate habit of sleeping slanted and taking up the whole damned bed, and the lower half of her body is crushing my legs and I fight the urge to kick her.

I become still again so I don't wake Paul and Rosemary yet. They'll immediately start talking, and then I won't be able to hear anything, and then my parents will know I'm awake and the rest of the day won't be this still, quiet peace that is rapidly drifting away from me.

I roll my eyes when I hear my parents arguing and I bite down on my lower lip, hard. I am so frustrated with them that whatever happiness I had knowing today was Christmas has left, along with the melting frost, all but gone from the window now.

I hear another noise, and then I hear the dogs whining and shaking their collars, and I realise my parents have let them into the house. I look down and Paul is opening his eyes. Damn. My peaceful little place is gone now. Paul feels Rosemary's legs on his too and he kicks her legs off him.

Rosemary wakes up and instantly starts to whine. Immediately I interrupt them both. 'It's Christmas you guys!'

They stop whining. The child-like look of wonder is quickly replaced by doubt as Paul looks at me and asks me, 'Are Mom and Dad awake? Can we get out of bed yet?' Before I can answer him, the bedroom door opens and our dogs run into the room, followed by Mom, smiling.

The dogs jump on the bed and roll all over us before jumping back down to the *floor and running all over the house. Paul and Rosemary jump out of bed, both of them managing to elbow and knee me in their excitement.*

Paul runs past Mom while Rosemary clings to her. I carefully examine Mom's face; no bruises, no tears. Apparently, whatever they were arguing about a few moments earlier wasn't very important, and I am relieved.

Mom ushers us into the bathroom where we brush our teeth and comb our hair. Now that we look acceptable, we can go into the living room where the presents and the Christmas tree are. We hug our father who is half awake, hair mussed up, a cup of coffee in his hand and his favourite green robe on.

'Oh no, breakfast first!' my father says as we run up to him to give him a hug. He's not really angry right now though, just half asleep. We sit at the table and even though Mom's cinnamon buns are amazing, we eat them at lightning speed so that we can go back into the living room. I mean,

really, what kid wants to eat first thing on Christmas Day?

We sit and fidget at the table until my dad is done eating. Halfway through his cinnamon bun, he looks up, sighs, picks up his plate and walks back into the living room, muttering to himself.

My father never looks quite right in pictures either. He never really smiles in them. It's a trained smile he gives for the camera, and it looks alien and uncomfortable on him.

Mom shoos us from the table, and Paul and Rosemary giggle and chase after my dad. I walk around the table and I kiss Mom on the cheek. 'Best cinnamon buns ever, Mom.' She smiles gratefully at me.

'You guys are holding up Christmas!' my dad yells. Mom and I head into the living room. Mom scolds Rosemary and Paul for being too hyper and tells them to sit quietly on the couch while she hands everyone one present at a time. We open them neatly and

slowly, in turn, so my parents can take pictures.

Rosemary usually gets to open a present first because she's the youngest, and she's whiny and fidgety sometimes, and my parents expect my brother and me to behave better than that. Today is no exception, and she's busy unwrapping a present while everyone else sits still and watches.

You have to act excited when you're opening presents. If you don't act excited enough, you could get yelled at. When you're done unwrapping your present, you can stare at it in awe for a few seconds before you have to hold it up for the rest of the family to see and take pictures while you smile. You can never not like a present, even if it's a hideous sweater two sizes too small that you will never ever wear.

Christmas is always like this for us. The day becoming ever more excruciating until Dad decides to take a nap and Mom starts cooking dinner. Then, and only sometimes, we stop acting like Stepford children and act like normal kids who squeal and rip through presents excitedly in a colourful tornado. For now the lie continues.

I look over at my dad and he's petting Noodles and talking to her softly. Noodles is wagging her curly little tail and sniffing his face. He scratches behind her velvet ears, ears that have been rubbed so much because of their softness that they're starting to go bald in spots.

I walk over, with the big brown blanket that I was wrapped in, and curl up next to my dad, who gives the dog a final pet and then wraps his arm around me. All is well right now, and I couldn't care less about the presents.

Rosemary squeals and holds up a doll. Mom takes pictures. Rosemary runs up to Mom and kisses her on the cheek and throws her little arms around Mom's neck. Mom whispers in her ear to hug her dad first next time she opens a present.

The Finer Points of Becoming...

Rosemary seems to baffle my father, and he is always slightly aloof with her. She's much more like a normal kid than my brother and me; she cries and whines and pretends, and gets my brother and me into trouble all the time. Her childlike nature confuses my dad, I think, and he doesn't know how to deal with her. She was a fussy baby who only wanted Mom to hold her, and cried whenever anyone else tried to pick her up, including my dad, who was so confused as to why his own child didn't want her dad to hold her that he finally quit trying.

Rosemary runs and quickly hugs my dad and thanks him. Dad pats her on the back and Rosemary runs to sit on the floor and play with her new doll. Mom picks out a present for Paul. Paul opens the present, which is some army action figure, and says 'wow, cool!' before posing for his picture. He runs over to my dad. Paul throws his arms around my dad who lets go of me and they start play wrestling.

My dad was always trying to toughen Paul up, even though he wasn't into sports or anything else considered manly. So when he showed an interest in action figures, my dad had no problem encouraging this new interest.

I sigh, jealous. I am a tomboy; I like sports and the outdoors and wrestling around and bows and arrows and guns. But I am not a boy, and though my dad will get frustrated with Paul and eventually start to play with me, he always wants to play with my brother first.

'Emmy, it's your turn.'

I look over at Mom, who has seen me being slighted by my father and calls me over to her. I open the small present, certain that it is a book. It is one from my favourite series, a science fiction book for adults. I never read children's books; I'm not allowed to. They are too retarded for me, my parents say. I am too smart to act like a child, they say. But they encourage my love of books, and Mom has gone through my bookshelf and found out which book I don't have, and has picked out the latest one.

I smile for my picture and hold my book up, and then hug Mom. Nobody is watching me. Rosemary is playing with her doll and Paul is still wrestling and laughing with my dad.

Mom and I sit on the floor, united in our sudden invisibility to the rest of the family. 'You picked the one I wanted Mommy. Thank you.'

Mom smiled, a soft sad smile. 'I know things aren't always easy for you and I uh...' she stopped and suddenly remembered how things had to be. '...I just wanted to get you the right one Emmy. Now go hug your dad.'

I walk up to my dad and hug him from behind. He looks slightly startled.

'Hey kid, what'd ya get?'

I show Dad the book.

'A book huh? Is it a good one?'

'Yeah Dad, it is.'

My dad stares at the book for a second. I have never seen my dad read a book. 'Well, good for you,' he finally says, and his eyes dart past me, past my book, and to Mom.

He stands up and goes to the tree and rummages around for a box wrapped in the comics section of the newspaper. He hands it to Mom, who smiles, kisses him and opens it. It is a cranberry-coloured sweater dress.

'I uh, ya know, thought that'd look good on you Teresa,' he says, suddenly unsure of himself.

I feel bad for my dad, who in the midst of his family, and this holiday, had felt... what? Ashamed that he hadn't wrapped the present as well as Mom had wrapped the others?

Suddenly he is a tired-looking man, beginning to look older than he should, unsure of himself amongst his own family. He's confused by books that his daughter reads — that I will later come to suspect he couldn't — confused by his son's femininity and his youngest daughter's apparent dislike of him, confused as to why his wife flinches every time he goes near her.

My father sits back down quickly and busies himself with drinking the last of his coffee. His vulnerability has disappeared and is replaced by his grey, distant stare, a faraway look that sometimes comes to his eyes and leaves you wondering where he wishes he would rather be.

Slowly, the rest of the presents are passed out, books and dolls and action figures, socks and sweaters and odd gifts, like a gallon of cheap drugstore bubble bath that Paul had saved his allowance for, so that he could give it to Mom for Christmas. Like any mother though, she loved it and hugged Paul, whose hazel eyes matched hers, and promised to use it that night.

That afternoon, after my dad lies down to sleep and while Paul and Rosemary are busy playing with their toys, I go into the kitchen with Mom to help her with dinner.

She brews another cup of coffee and pours me a half-cup for helping her. We sit and peel potatoes and carrots together, whispering and laughing quietly, sometimes so much that we have to cover our faces with dishtowels so we won't be too loud and possibly wake my father. Mom puts the towel in her lap and wipes a tear of laughter away. She hugs me and smiles.

'Oh, Emmy. You're my best friend Emmy.'

I smile back at her. 'You're mine too, Mom.'

CHAPTER 9
Paying attention

I'm sitting in Dr X's office, waiting. I yawn and look around his office, bored and tired. His desk is piled high with papers and patient folders, which surprises me somewhat. Every other time I've been in this office it's been neat and tidy.

When he finally comes into the office, he looks flustered and tired. 'Good morning, Emma. I'm sorry I'm late, but we had some patients come in early this morning...'

He trails off and sits down behind his desk, trying to organise the paperwork there. He settles for putting it all in a pile on the right side of his desk.

I wait. He looks at me. My hands are neatly crossed in my lap, not over my chest like they usually are. He doesn't seem to notice.

'So Emma, how are you? No, wait. I need to get your file; just a moment...'

He begins to sift through the stack of folders and papers on his desk. His brow furrows and he mutters to himself until he finds it. He wipes it off, opens it up, and starts glancing over it. He nods to himself and looks back up at me.

'I hear you had a hard time at dinner last night, Emma. Is there a reason why?' He picks up his pen, waiting for my response.

I'm slightly surprised by his question. 'Uh, what do you mean?' I ask.

'Well, according to the evening nurse, you didn't want to eat dinner last night. She made a note of it. Now again, is there a reason you didn't want to eat last night, Emma?'

'Um, well kind of. The food was gross, and I didn't like it.'

Dr X looks at me suspiciously.

'I'm serious.' I tell him. He continues to look at me without speaking. 'I mean, the food was cold *and* burnt at the same time, and I'm not a big fan of meatloaf. I just didn't like dinner.'

'So it was a food preference issue, and not anything else?' he asks me.

'Yup,' I nod. 'That's it. Nothing else.'

Dr X looks at me, and I'm not quite sure he believes me, but he accepts my response.

'Well Emma, I must remind you that you're very thin, and that with the different medications you're on...'

I zone out. I don't really mean to, but I just click into autopilot, nodding my head as he continues talking about needing to eat and how if I don't, it affects how the medications get into my system or something like that. I'm busy staring at a picture of Dr X with a beautiful, well-dressed blonde woman, holding an infant.

'What did I just say Emma?' Dr X asks me.

'Uh…' I stammer. 'You said it's important to follow the rules because if I don't, it affects my treatment.' I tell him.

I wasn't paying attention, and I'm not entirely sure that's what he was talking about, but that's become my stock answer any time someone starts talking about something that I'm not interested in hearing, and usually it works out. Today, it doesn't.

'Yes, and then I said that a third leg was growing out of your stomach, to see if you were paying attention. And then you nodded and agreed with me.' Dr X tells me.

Damn. I'm caught. I look down and snicker in spite of myself. Dr X seems offended by my snickering. '*What* are you laughing about, Emma?' He's irritated now.

'I'm sorry. The third leg thing was funny,' I say sheepishly. The humour of his comment seems to escape him until I point it out and despite himself, he cracks a smile briefly before clearing his throat and resuming his usual clinical demeanour.

'Yes well, never mind. How are you feeling today?' Now he picks up his pen to take notes.

I think for a minute. Really, I'm trying to figure out what I'm going to say, so that I'm not telling him too much but not being so vague as to let him know that I'm evading his questions.

'Um, ya know, trying to get used to the medication and stuff...' and I continue to talk about how I'm trying to deal with my parents' divorce and how it upset me, when Dr X's beeper goes off. He frowns and takes it off his belt, looking at the number before he sighs and interrupts me.

'I'm sorry Emma, we're going to have to continue this later. I hate to interrupt you, but I have to go. Uh, just keep writing in your journal and following your uh, treatment plan.'

He grabs a stack of folders and rushes to the door before he turns and looks at me. 'I'm really sorry Emma,' he says.

I realise he feels bad and I smile to make him feel better. 'It's cool Doc,' I tell him. He shakes his head and rushes out the door.

I pick up my journal and follow him out of the office to join everyone else in the common room. It's visiting time. Cindy walks out of the visiting room laughing and giggling, her parents are behind her. They tearfully hug, and Cindy waves to her parents as they leave.

I glare at Cindy and start drawing little spiral designs on the cover of my journal, irritated with her for being happier than I am. I open my journal and I read what I'd written in it; *You will not reach me.*

I frown and start chewing on my fingernails as I re-read those words over and over again. I had decided when I got to this hell hole of group therapy, bad food, and dingy walls, that I didn't need help.

I look down at my arms and back at the words. I tap my pencil on my journal, deep in thought. I finally stop tapping and start to write.

December ??

I wrote the words 'You will not reach me' on the inside of my journal when I got here. Why? What point was I trying to prove, and to whom? That I'm OK, that I don't need anybody? I think maybe I was wrong.

I look at the journal entry and try to decide just where I'm going with this. A thought is starting to dawn on me, that I'm not exactly doing OK. How do I fix it though? I put the pencil back to the paper and continue writing.

I'm not sure what exactly it is that I'm trying to say, other than that I was wrong about not needing help. I still think everyone here is retarded, and Dr X is too busy to help me the way I probably need to be helped, but now I realise that everything that happened with my parents really did affect me more than I thought it did, and I need to do something about it.

My pencil snaps. 'Dammit!' I glare at the offending pencil. I sigh and pick up my journal in irritation, clutching it tightly to my chest as I walk over to the main desk where the nurses and orderlies are busy discussing the events of some television show that I have never watched and don't care about.

'Hey, can I have another pencil?' I ask, and show the pencil to the group. Without really paying any attention to me, an orderly puts a pencil on the counter and continues talking to the rest of the group. 'Oh I know! I can't believe that happened on the show! I was like, oh, no way...'

I roll my eyes, pick up the pencil and walk off, muttering to myself as I walk back to my chair. 'Stupid people and their stupid fake lives and stupid TV shows...'

I start tapping on my paper with the new pencil and I try to remember what I was writing about. I'm having a hard time remembering, the meds are clouding my brain and making it hard to hold onto a thought.

'Hey Emma! What's going on?' Ricky's voice interrupts me again and I drop the pencil onto the journal. I furrow my brow and I begin to rub the bridge of my nose as I close my eyes.

'Hi Ricky. I'm kind of um, ya know, thinking about stuff.'

Ricky looks like I just told him that I hated him.

'Oh. OK. Well, I just, ya know, wanted to see if you were doing OK. You seemed kind of out of it yesterday.' Ricky toes the ground dejectedly.

I feel bad. I don't want to tell Ricky to go away, but it seems like he has the absolute *worst* timing ever. I decide to compromise.

'Oh yeah. Hey Ricky, that was really nice of you to check on me last night. I really appreciate it.'

Ricky smiles. 'Uh, no problem Emma. It's cool. I think you're really nice and I was worried, so I wanted to make sure that you know that you can talk to me any time.' He laughs nervously and toes the ground again, and I inwardly groan as I start to get the disturbing feeling that Ricky has a crush on me.

'Uh yeah. I got it. Thanks Ricky. I'm gonna go back to writing now, OK? Dr X wants me to uh, ya know, write more and all, so I don't want to get into trouble or anything.'

'Uh, OK Emma. See ya later.' Ricky walks away. I wrinkle my nose at him before I go to my journal.

Where was I? I tap the pencil thoughtfully on my lower lip. Thoughts are swirling like fog, and I can't seem to latch onto any one of them now. My concentration is broken again, as laughter from the main desk seeps into my ears.

'Goddamned normal people and their stupid conversations...' I start muttering to myself and a thought begins to solidify in my head, a conversation with myself.

Are you mad at them for watching television, or are you mad at them because they're laughing? That's it, isn't it? You're mad at them because they're not like you. They're not in here because they can't live with the darkness in their heads, it's a job to them. They haven't lived your life, and you hate them for having something you didn't have; a seemingly normal life with a normal job and normal friends. You're bitter, and that's just sad, hating other people because you're jealous. And that's what you boil down to, isn't it? A bitter, sad, unhappy, not-quite-little-any-more girl. If you don't cut the crap Emma, and start dealing with what's really making you unhappy...

What's really making me unhappy? I sigh and write down the answer to this painful question.

I am unhappy because of my parents.

The words are simple, but they say so much more than that to me. I read them and realise that I'm beginning to come face to face with the years of abuse I watched and grew up with. I don't know how to fix what's wrong with me, but as I look around this room, I know that I don't want to be in this place any more. Not just in this room, but in this place inside myself, this place of fear and guilt for things in the past that I couldn't control.

I could not control what happened to me. It was not my fault.

My eyes blur as I read what I've just written. I've been blaming myself for what my mom went through, for not being able to protect her from my father; for Paul and Rosemary growing up watching the same abuse that I was watching, and being unable to do anything about it. I've always thought that it was my fault, that if I had been stronger or older, I could have stopped what was going on around me.

I have turned all my fear and disgust into guilt, and it's been twisting inside of me until I can't even breathe. I'm starting to realise that the night I ended up in the hospital wasn't really about Donnie breaking up with me.

Sure it hurt, losing Donnie. We had a lot of fun together, and he was hot. Plus, it was nice having a boyfriend who could buy booze. But when he broke up with me, all I wanted was for my mom to show me that she cared, and she couldn't, or wouldn't, do it. All I had really wanted was someone to love me.

I sit in the chair, trying to decide what I am going to do with all these new thoughts and realisations that are coming to me.

I've spent years telling myself that I am a machine, that I can't feel, just to let me cope with the horrors happening around me.

'Emma.' A voice startles me.

'Huh?'

Ricky is standing next to me. Before I have the chance to bitch him out for interrupting my newborn thoughts, he says 'Emma, they want you at the front desk.'

'For what?' I complain.

'I don't know. They've been calling you.' Ricky shrugs and walks off.

'Goddamned lazy stupid nurses...' I start bitching and angrily snatch up my journal and pencil and storm to the desk. The nurses and orderlies are still busy having some painfully normal conversation about whatever it is normal people talk about.

'Uh, someone was calling for me?' I ask when I get to the front desk.

A chunky, bald, twenty-something male orderly looks up at me. 'What do ya want?' he says, smacking the gum in his mouth loudly.

I frown. 'I don't know. Someone up here was calling me.'

'And who are you?'

'Emma. Emma Banks.'

His expression turns to one of recognition. 'Oh yeah, got a visitor here for you.'

I hope it's Mom. 'Who is it?' I ask.

The orderly looks down at the sign-in sheet, still smacking the gum around in his mouth.

'Uhhhh...' he says as he reads down the list.

I tap my foot impatiently.

'Banks, Emma... uhh...'

'Yes. Emma Banks,' I snap at him.

'Banks... Banks... Sorry about that. Uh yeah, it looks like your father is here to see you.'

'My step-dad?' I ask him, confused. The orderly checks the list again.

'Uh, his name is Austin Banks.' The orderly reads the name from the sheet. 'Just wait here and someone will escort you into the visiting room in just a sec.'

He sits down and rejoins the conversation, leaving me standing, speechless.

The blood drains from my face and my feet feel cemented to the ground. My head starts to spin.

'Oh shit.' I whisper to myself, and suddenly I'm shaking and can't seem to stop.

Austin Banks is my father.

CHAPTER 10

The family legend and the rise of the machine

As I sit in the hallway, I start chewing nervously on my nails. I'm waiting to be escorted into the visiting room where my father sits, also waiting.

Why has he come here? Is he here to yell at me? To criticise me? Can I refuse his visit? Do I *want* to?

No. If he is here to talk to me, then I'll try to see him and find out just what *has* brought him here. I wonder if I'll always suspect his motives now. Possibly. Probably.

In my mind I see his face, and though I recognise the features, they are cold and lifeless and waxy, like an exhibit in a museum. When I think of him like this, I don't think of him as Dad, or even my father at all; I think of him as Austin, someone remote from me, someone I don't have to care about who doesn't have to care about me. But Austin really is my father's name.

I know very little about my father's life before he met my mother. From the bits and pieces I've been able to gather together over the years, I know that he grew up on a farm in a small town, and spent more time working on the farm than going to school. He had several siblings, all of whom died very young in slightly suspicious accidents, such as drowning in the bathtub, or falling into a washing machine. Leaves you thinking that Austin was lucky to survive whatever was happening with that family of his. His own father left Austin and his mother while Austin was young. His mother got married again, to a rigid, abusive, and uncaring man. This is how the family legend goes...

The clock seems to have slowed down so much as to be standing still. I'm still here, waiting to see the man who had helped create me, for better or for worse. A curious mix of fear, love, and curiosity overtakes me. I am not totally comfortable. Then the meds just happen to kick in. For the first time I am grateful for them, knowing that they'll keep me calm so that I won't freak out in the visiting room. And now, alongside the waxy head of Austin, I'm seeing in my thoughts the waxy, emotionless stare of Teresa. Teresa, my mother.

Austin graduated high school and moved to the city, where he met Teresa. This much I've been told – over and over it seems. More of the family legend. Teresa had lived through problems of her own, and at the tender age of eighteen had already spent most of her adolescent and young adult life working multiple jobs. She'd had to support herself and her own mother – an alcoholic, manic depressive, abusive mess...

At last, the same bald orderly who had told me that my father was here to see me gets up from the desk. He grabs the keys and escorts me to the visiting room.

I take a deep breath and walk into the room. My dad – *Austin* – is sitting there, looking through a Bible. He looks up at me and stands and I can't feel my legs holding me upright, even though they are.

'Hi Emmy,' he finally says.

'Hi Dad,' I answer. It's all I *can* say right now.

The door shuts behind us.

Austin was in his early twenties when he met Teresa at the diner where she worked her night job. She was charmed by his accent and quick wit; he loved her hard-working attitude and shyness.

They were married six weeks later in a

tiny chapel, with only a handful of guests.

Three months into their marriage, Teresa became pregnant with her first child. I was born seven months later, a tiny, pale, sickly baby. Austin got a job in a factory and worked long hours to provide for his new family.

I've seen pictures of me and Dad when I was a baby, and I can tell by the way he held me that I was a precious, fragile, breakable thing to him, and that he loved me dearly...

We sit in uncomfortable silence for what seems like forever, but in reality is probably only a minute or so. My father speaks first. He sees my arms and he stares, hard, before his eyes meet mine.

'Oh Emma, what the hell did you do to yourself kid?' he asks me, and his voice seems sad. And there's still so much running through my head.

Most of the fights in the beginning were caused by the stress any young married couple feels when the money is too low and the bills are too high. Teresa took on sewing jobs from a local tailor shop to help bring money in.

Teresa became pregnant again, and two years after I was born, Paul came into the world.

I've been told that the fighting got worse around this time. The family legend. But Mom was young, had no money, and nowhere to go with two children aged two and under, even if she had wanted to leave. She stayed, and five months after Paul was born, she became pregnant with Rosemary.

Sitting opposite him, I am surprised by my dad's tone. I am so used to hearing him angry or upset with me that he completely catches me off guard. My eyes well up with tears. I try to fumble for an explanation.

'I, uh, hurt myself Dad,' is all I can manage to get out.

'Emma, honey... why?' he asks. Again he surprises me with the concern in his voice.

What can I say? How can I explain to him, especially with him acting so nice with me right now, that it is partially his fault that I am here in the first place? How can I tell him that the years of fighting and abuse has festered inside my head until it has become an infection, one that is killing me? I can't, so I sit and suffer in silence. This is something I've done often enough. We all have. Me and Paul and Rosemary.

I don't remember Paul — or even Rosemary — being born. But I can remember bits and pieces of things shortly after that. No longer just family legend; I know this for real.

I remember one time, my dad had an old motorcycle that he spent a lot of time fixing up, polishing and working on. One day he and Mom were fighting over God knows what, and he looked at me, picked me up, and we went out to the garage. He sat on the motorcycle and sat me behind him, using a belt to secure me to his back.

We rode and rode until we were in a forest somewhere. He stopped the bike, and we got off and walked into a tiny log-cabin convenience store at the base of a trail. My dad bought me apple juice in a little glass bottle that was shaped like an apple, and we bought beef jerky.

We followed the trail until we came to a little stream, with stepping stones placed so you could get to the other side. When we were walking across, I remember slipping and I fell in. My dad turned around and started laughing as he picked me up, all cold and wet and startled. I started to laugh too, and he kissed me on the head and said 'Emma, don't you know how to walk?'

He carried me the rest of the way back to the motorcycle, wrapping me up in his *sweatshirt. We rode home to where Mom was waiting, none too happy to see me dishevelled and sopping wet. They immediately got into an argument over how long my father had been gone, and what in the hell was he doing with a child that young on the back of a motorcycle anyway?*

My father sits in silence, like he's unsure of what to say next. I've always felt that he is made out of stone, a living, breathing statue. His sudden concern for me is shaking me to the core. I'm scared because I feel I'm starting to doubt everything that I've ever thought about him over the years. Then he finds his voice again.

'I brought you this Emma,' he says, and hands me the Bible in his hands. It is burgundy, leather bound, and in the bottom right hand corner he's had my name imprinted on it. I am touched, even if right now I have a hard time even believing that God exists, much less cares about me.

'I don't understand what's going on Emma, but I, uh, thought this might help you.'

'Thanks Dad,' is all I can say. I place the Bible gingerly in my lap, not sure what else to do with it. More awkward silence.

My dad was impulsive. One day, he came home with a cream-coloured, wrinkled dog that we named Noodles. He showed us the dog first, so Mom couldn't make him take it back when she saw how much we wanted to keep it. Mom resented the dog at first, but she grew to love the protective and ever so patient, wrinkly, smelly little thing.

I think that I remember the fights getting worse around that time too, or maybe I just started to see what was really happening around me.

At first they always fought when we were in the other room, but gradually they started to fight in front of us. And that's when the fear started creeping into me and wouldn't let go.

I had nightmares, constantly. Until I was nearly ten years old, I begged to sleep in my parents' room every night. When they finally wouldn't let me sleep with them any more, I slept with the light on.

The effect my parents' fighting had on us kids began to show in other ways too. Paul was having a hard time potty training, and would often wet the bed in his sleep. Mom and I tried to hide it from Dad. But he found out anyway, and hit Paul to teach him not to be lazy, and to go to the bathroom at night.

As for Rosemary, she had the annoying habit of crying constantly and throwing fits. She also had a very vivid imagination. Cute in a child, it developed to become uncontrollable lying.

In addition to not being able to sleep, I began to have problems eating. My stomach was constantly in knots, and I remained pale and thin. And I would cry at the worst possible times, like in front of my classmates if I got an answer wrong at school...

I've been lost in these thoughts in the cold silence of the visitor room. My dad, speaking, brings me back.

'Emma... Why did you do this to yourself? Why didn't you call me?'

Ugh. The question I've been dreading. If I want to answer honestly, I'll say something like '...because I'm so afraid of you that I couldn't tell you that anything was wrong. And because Mom didn't want you to try to take me away from her...' But of course, those words aren't going to come out of my mouth, so I settle for a half-truth.

'Because Dad, um, you know, we haven't got along real well for the past few years, and I didn't think you'd want to hear from me.'

My dad looks surprised at first, then shakes his head.

'Kid, I know we haven't always got along, but I never wanted anything bad to happen to you. You're my little girl. Do you know how upset everyone is that you're in here right now?'

'Yes Dad, I know,' I reply, dropping my head. Even in his concern, he is still making me feel bad. Like I have just been selfish in trying to kill myself.

...through all the troubles my father began to work more and more, and eventually got promoted in his job. But even though he was making more money, his family was falling apart. And he began to fall apart with the pressure of everything. So he clamped down on us, thinking that a tighter grip would fix everything. We, at least, should be something that he could control. Then when he finally realised that that wasn't working, he just blamed Mom.

It became a fact of daily life, just like waking up and brushing your teeth, that my parents would fight, that my mom would cry and that my dad would hit her.

And sometimes he'd hit us. But it didn't necessarily happen in that order.

I'm thinking, remembering, but I'm on full alert just sitting there, ready to listen when I have to.

My dad continues, unaware that anything is running through my head. 'Do you have any idea what it was like for me to get a phone call saying that you were in this...' he looks around distastefully '...place?'

Again, I feel ashamed at being here. I don't say anything. And then I feel his eyes staring at me. He is expecting a response.

'No Dad. I don't know what it was like for you. I'm sorry.'

Our relationship is always going to be like this, I think to myself. I am never going to be good enough, smart enough, pretty enough, or well behaved enough to make him proud of me.

At school I was the weird kid, and since I had no friends and my home life was miserable, I began to escape into books. I was fascinated with a character in one of my science fiction books. An android. I loved how he didn't feel anything, how he was so human but didn't have the same pesky emotions that I couldn't seem to control within myself.

I decided that I wanted to be an android. Whenever I got upset, I would repeat certain phrases to myself, over and over and over again, like a mechanical thing, until I felt calm and emotionless and in control once more.

And if I couldn't control my home life, I could control other things; like whether I ate or not, or even whether I wanted to have feelings for anything at all.

The worse the fighting got, the less I ate and the less I allowed myself to feel. In exasperation one day, my mom finally started screaming at me and crying, 'What is wrong with you Emma? You're like a machine; you don't eat, you don't feel, you don't smile. What is wrong?'

My dad runs his hands through his hair and sighs deeply. I wonder if maybe he knows that I hadn't been thinking of what kind of phone call he'd get when I was admitted to this place. I don't want to dwell on that though. Thankfully, he changes the subject.

'Jesus Emma, you look like hell. They have you all doped up, don't they? What do they have you on?'

I try to remember the names of the medications, but my mind is swirling from the meds and from sitting in this room with him. I just can't remember. I begin to panic when I realise that I am unable to answer his question, and I start to hyperventilate.

Back to my memories, back to my memories, back to my memories. They finally tired of fighting all the time and I started to see the change in my mother. Despite the bruises, she had reached the point where either she was going to die, or he was.

When I was thirteen, they sat us down at the table and told us that they couldn't get along any more, and that they thought it was best for everyone if they got a divorce. They said something about how they had agreed to disagree and told us that everything was going to be fine. Just words, telling us that they'd take care of us and not put us in the middle, and that it wasn't our fault. I actually thanked God when they told me the news. At least I had the hope that something was going to change.

And oh, change did happen. My father threw my mother out of the house with nothing more than the clothes on her back. We didn't see her except on the weekends, and more often than not, my father would make one of us stay behind to keep him company.

My parents kept fighting though, and it became scary. One minute my father *was drunk and screaming death threats at my mother, the next day they had decided to call off the divorce and pretend like we were suddenly going to become some perfect family. It never lasted. It would all fall apart a few weeks later in some new violent and dramatic argument. Repeat* ad nauseam.

It came to the point where they hated each other so much that they tried to push their hatred of each other on us. I never bought it though, which pissed them both off. I couldn't understand why they, as adults, couldn't understand that I loved both of them.

I became more and more isolated from them, and they both began to treat me more as a problem – and occasionally, as a weapon – than their child...

I'm still hyperventilating a little, and my dad is grabbing my shoulder and making me look at him.

'Emma, calm down. Breathe. I'll ask the nurses about the medication, it's not a big deal, OK?'

But it *is* a big deal; he just doesn't know it. He's never taken a long look at himself. Before the divorce, when we all lived together, you had to answer every question with quick, concise answers. You got into trouble if you didn't.

As I grew older, I began to drink and date older guys. Looking back on my behaviour now, I'm sure that I was seeking the love that my father wouldn't or couldn't give me, from older men. And I was in so much pain – despite all my best efforts to be a machine – that I needed to numb myself. So I chose to do that through drinking.

My father began drinking heavily round about this time too. He was drunk constantly, and would see-saw emotionally. He would go from being depressed at losing his family, to angry, to hitting the bars and bringing home random women. Just so that he wouldn't be lonely. We began to fight even more as his behaviour became more and more intolerable. He refused to pay a penny of child support, so my mom, my sister and I were practically starving in our apartment. Just the three of us at this time; Paul went to live with his father...

I start to slow my breathing down and clutch the Bible in my lap with an iron grip, in an effort to hide my shaking hands from my dad.

He starts to talk again, like he thinks that the sound of his voice will make things better. At least he talks about something different.

'How are they treating you, kid? Do you have enough to eat?'

'Yes Dad.'

'Is the food OK?'

Apparently I make a face, and he cracks a smile, the first smile I've seen on his face since I walked into this tomb-like room.

'Apparently, that's a no then,' he says.

'Uh, yeah. The food sucks.'

My dad frowns at my use of the word *sucks*. Again, fear washes over me as I wait to get backhanded for saying a *bad* word. But no backhand comes.

The separation was hard on everybody, and it just got harder. My dreams of some peace once my parents finally divorced were shattered when my father, in a drunken rage, threatened to kill a pet rabbit that belonged to Rosemary. Now fifteen years old, and aged beyond my years, I jumped between him and my sister and told him to go to bed and sober up. He looked at me in absolute shock for about three seconds before he started screaming at me at the top of his lungs, about two inches from my face.

'DON'T TELL ME HOW TO RAISE MY KIDS!' he screamed.

'Then raise them so that I don't HAVE to.'

When he hit me, I hit him back. Rosemary was bawling and hyperventilating behind me, huddled in a corner of the kitchen. I picked her up and went to the phone and called my mom. She came right away and picked us up. We didn't see much more of him after that...

It's strange to see my father sitting across the room from me now. He looks completely baffled, so that I almost think he's noticed how scared I've become.

'Emma, why are you so jumpy?'

It dawns on me that he is completely unaware of the effect his presence has on me. Jesus, he really has no clue as to what all the years of fighting and yelling did to us – Mom, Paul, Rosemary and me.

Again I'm asking myself; 'Do I tell him the truth, or do I just try to get through this meeting with as much grace as I can muster?'

I settle for the latter. 'Uh, it's the meds I think, Dad. I'm not used to taking them and I'm a little jumpy because of it.' I can lie to him without even thinking.

My father remarried a year later. She was a nice blonde woman who had a son of her own. He moved away with her, and with Paul, to a city a few hours away from where we lived.

Mom also remarried. Daniel was a kindly man she met at work. Rosemary and I fell in love with him instantly. He had big arms that made you feel safe when he hugged you, and a laugh that was warm and friendly. Best of all, he loved and took care of my mom. That was all I wanted.

I thought things would be better after that, but I still couldn't get past the things going on in my head, residue from all the fighting and fear that just wouldn't go away.

I started to cut myself and my mom found out. She took me to a psychologist who prescribed pills for me and wanted to talk about the divorce. I didn't want to talk about the divorce, so my mom told the psychologist about my father when I wouldn't answer his questions...

My dad stares at me, hard. That stare cuts through me, and I can swear that he knows that I am lying, telling him about the pills making me jumpy. But if he does know, he's not saying anything. For now.

'So, uh...' he begins. He's searching for words to connect us, but not finding any beyond those. Neither of us knows what to say.

Not wanting to sit in yet more awkward silence, I jump in and ask him questions. I'm hoping to move the spotlight away from me in this way too.

'How is your wife, uh, Julie, doing?' I ask.

'She's fine. But she's worried about you. I wish you'd give her a chance, kiddo. She's a real nice lady.'

'Uh, yeah. She seems nice.'

The truth of the matter is, Julie *is* a nice woman. My resentment towards her comes from the fact that my dad seems to treat her so much better than he treated Mom. Because of that, I've wanted nothing to do with Julie. I am bitter and jealous, resentful of his love and concern for her. I am polite with her, but that is it.

...Mom, Rosemary and me, we all moved up to Daniel's house after he and Mom got married. I should have been happy but it was never that simple. It still isn't. I met Donnie at a football game that I'd attended solely to get out of the house. Anything would do, just to be able to get drunk and smoke pot without my parents knowing. From that point it was mostly drink and drugs and Donnie that I cared about. The break up with Donnie

was, of course, like the straw that broke my back. It's why I'm here. In this place. Sitting across from my father...

'Julie wanted to come see you, but she didn't think that you wanted to see her,' my dad says pointedly. He has no way of knowing what I've been thinking about. All the same, I'd better pay attention. I still don't know if I can trust him.

'Uh, sorry Dad. I just... I'm not real proud that I'm in here, and um, don't want anyone to see me like this. I don't want to embarrass you.'

'Well, that's understandable, I suppose,' he finally concedes. 'It'd be nice if you'd come to visit us more. After you get out of here I mean, Emma. I'm your dad, and I miss you.'

I am suspicious of his motives for wanting me to come visit. I am sure that he wants to show me off to Julie; show her how well behaved and intelligent and adult-like I am. God knows why he'd think I would be. But I just agree with him anyway.

'OK Dad. I'll come visit more.'

I really have no intention of visiting him more, though, and I know that if I tell my mom I don't want to go, most likely she won't make me. I am lying again, but it's best this way. We'll just end up in an argument, and that is the last thing that I want. What I really *do* want is for this awkward visit to end. Even though my dad is being nice, I'm not over the years when he *wasn't* nice. I'm not over the bruises and the hurtful words, and the lying and covering up his abusive nature to the outside world. I can't stop being suspicious.

My dad starts talking about work, about Julie, about his step-son Russ, and how ill-behaved Russ is. That most likely means that Russ is just a *normal* kid. I know how that would infuriate my father.

I figure that we are just about winding down the visit when my dad hits me with a whammy.

'So, I heard about your incident with the nurse, Emma.'

I wince. Here it comes, I think. He's going to yell at me and make me feel worthless. I brace myself and stare at the floor.

'I'm not really sure what the hell has got into you Emma, but you need to get your shit together, kid.'

I nod in agreement with him, which is what I know he wants. 'Yes Dad. I'm trying.'

'It's almost Christmas, Emma,' he says, changing the subject again.

'Yeah, I know Dad.' I bite my lower lip to keep myself from crying.

'You don't want to be in here for Christmas, do you Emma?'

'No Dad, I don't.'

'We're going to have a big celebration at the house. We got you some presents, and I've already talked to your mom. She says you can come by for part of the day. *If* you get out of here in time.'

I look up, confused. My dad continues.

'What I'm saying, Emma...' he leans closer towards me '...is that you tell these damned doctors whatever it is that they want to hear, just so you can get out of this place. Got it? Just agree with them, so that we can take you home.'

I blink. My dad isn't concerned so much with me getting out of here and *being well*; he is just concerned with me getting *out*. As far as he is concerned – or so it seems – there is nothing wrong with me. There's no reason for me to be in this place. And the embarrassment he feels is oh-so real.

I finally nod my head. 'OK Dad.'

My dad nods too, and leans back in his chair. Suddenly, he looks at his watch and I know that he has other, more important places to be. He's ready to leave now.

'I gotta get going kid. Just remember this little talk, OK? I love you Emma.'

'I love you too, Dad.'

And that is it. He stands up, gives me a quick hug, and he walks out the door. I'm left sitting in stunned silence.

I whisper softly to myself. 'OK Emma. You heard him. Time to get out.'

The family legend is not pretty. But legends mean nothing to a machine.

CHAPTER 11
Time to get out of here

As I sit at the lunch table, my mind is preoccupied with thoughts of the meeting with my father. I'm not sure whether I should consider it a dismal failure or not. I hadn't said much of anything; what I had said was so edited before I spoke, that it felt like I had sat there and lied to him the entire time.

He had confused me, that's for sure. Instead of yelling at me, which I was sure he was going to do, he had appeared concerned for me. Questions still lingered in my head though. Was he really concerned about me, or was he concerned with the family image?

My mom had already told me that I had embarrassed the entire family by putting myself in here. And she had made sure to ask me not to say too much to anyone about the past.

How am I supposed to get better if I don't confront the past though? Does my trying to get better even matter to any of them any more?

Maybe it's just me. I absent-mindedly push the semi-frozen peas around on my plate, thinking – not for the first time – that maybe I should just get over it.

Everyone else seems to be doing fine since the divorce. Both of my parents have remarried. Paul is in the track team at his school, and Rosemary has joined the cheerleading squad. Their grades are improving, and they seem happy. Unlike me, still tormented with horrible memories of the past.

So why can't I be happy? Why am I busy drinking, smoking, starving myself? Why am I still up almost all night, every night, unable to sleep? Why do I refuse to appear to be even *close* to normal?

While everyone else in my family is thriving like flowers after a heavy rain, I am drowning. Still. The divorce has simply removed me from the situation; it has done nothing to remove the hurt, the way I thought it would.

I suddenly feel stupid and selfish. Once again, I feel like I am back at square one, trying to figure out what the hell is wrong with me. And trying to figure out why I can't get over something that everyone else in my family seems to have put behind them. At the very least, they seem able to pretend that the horrible past had never happened in the first place.

I am an embarrassment to my family. I know by now that everyone at school will know what has happened to me. When (if) I return, I won't be able to walk down the hallway without more whispers behind my back. I can see it now: 'Did you hear what

Emma did to herself?' they'll say. And the story would evolve and grow until it's nowhere near the truth. No matter – I can never tell them the truth anyway.

I sigh heavily. The meeting with my father is still confusing me, to put it mildly. Maybe he has changed. Maybe he and Mom just weren't meant to be together, and now that he's with this new, nice woman everything is OK. I suddenly feel like a jerk for refusing to visit him and his new wife.

Regardless of my confusion about my father and his motives for visiting me, he had at least said something that I agree with. '...Get out of here.'

I am tired of being in this shitty place, with its shitty food and fucked-up people. I begin to focus on the idea of getting out of here.

Get out. What is it going to take to prove that I can leave this place? I've already caused a scene, and the hospital is keeping me here until I show 'substantial progress'. So what exactly do they mean by 'substantial progress'?

I am going to have to lie my ass off to get out of here. Lying to the other patients, the nurses and the orderlies shouldn't be too hard. But I am worried about Dr X.

Dr X has already shown me that he will not buy most of the half-truths and lies that I tell everyone else. So if I do just all of a sudden start to act like everything is OK, he'll definitely grow suspicious of me. And keep me here even longer.

Dr X presents a problem, one that I'm not quite sure how to deal with just yet.

I finish eating and put my tray away. I chew on my fingernails, deep in thought. Suddenly, an idea comes to me. Dr X had been so flustered during the past few days that our meetings have seemed to run on autopilot. He has appeared tired and overworked. I wonder if I can use that to my advantage...

The reality is, I am in a county mental hospital that is overcrowded and understaffed, and needs the space for a seemingly constant stream of new arrivals. Surely I can work that, along with Dr X's tiredness, to my advantage. A few days of tearing up at group therapy and pretending to confess my deepest hurts and thoughts just might help persuade them that I am ready to change, that I am becoming what they want me to be.

I frown. I feel like I am going to be selling out. I am completely against the idea of acting like every other person in here. Half of them are in here seeking attention, and I hate them with every fibre of my being. The other half consists of genuine whack-jobs who have been in here for weeks.

I finally decide that it isn't selling out, just saying whatever I need to say to get myself out of here. I tell myself that it is a mission, and no different than lying to my teachers at school about why I'd missed class. Or lying to my mom, so she won't find out that I *have* missed class.

This is going to be trickier than just lying to a few teachers though. A plan is slowly forming in my head. The first thing I'll need to do is to quit playing little *games*, like the one where I stare at people until they feel uncomfortable. This thought depresses me. I am bored and lonely in here and my games are keeping me entertained. But then again, maybe they're helping keep me stuck in this place.

I'll have to stop colouring and painting pictures with black and red on everything. I'll have to participate more in the group sessions. I roll my eyes at the thought. Instantly I chastise myself for it. How am I supposed to get out of here if I can't even control my thoughts when nobody is looking?

I'll have to quit ignoring the schoolwork they assign us. I'll have to stop sulking in the back of the classroom, and pay attention. I'll have to stop rolling my eyes and saying as little as is humanly possible in the group therapy sessions. In short, I'll have to start acting like a normal kid who really wants to get better. And I'll have to keep it up until they think I actually *am* doing better. I'll have to start following the joke of a treatment plan that I've never really bothered to read.

I go to my room and dig the treatment plan out from a stack of other papers that I also haven't bothered to read. Dr X has given me pamphlets on depression, on rebuilding your life after a suicide attempt, and various other lame subjects.

I look at the treatment plan and figure that it is most likely a generic form, handed out to everybody. It has been photocopied so many times that there are black dots on the paper and the writing has become difficult to make out. With some effort, I begin to read what is written on the crumpled paper. There is a laundry list of generic things to do to help with depression and/or suicidal tendencies.

'Journal... yeah, I got that...' I read aloud to myself. 'Develop a hobby that will help you deal with stress in a constructive way, such as painting or gardening...' I scoff. Gardening. Who the hell does gardening anyway?

After some thought, I decide that it doesn't really matter; all I have to say is that when I get out of here, I *plan* to have a hobby. Fine. I'll tell them that I am going to continue drawing, since I have a mild interest in it anyway.

I continue reading the treatment plan. 'Make a list of trusted friends or family members that you can talk to openly and honestly.' I start to laugh. I can't talk openly and honestly to *anyone* in my family. Either they pretend that nothing is wrong, or they really *believe* that nothing is wrong. And the few times I have tried to talk about the way I grew up my mother either gets upset and defensive, or she changes the subject. I finally grew tired of making her cry, so I quit talking about my childhood to her altogether. That leaves me with friends, then. But when I think about my friends, I am stuck there, too.

The circle of friends I have consists of punk rockers, stoners, and other social misfits. They will discuss with a passion why a band sucks or not, but rarely discuss feelings. Unless the discussion involves a general discontent with being in high school and having a curfew.

Once again though, it doesn't really matter if I have friends and family I can talk to. To get out of here, I have to pretend that I have people I can talk to.

I think back to when my mom took me to therapy, and instantly I become irritated. Even in the therapist's office, I wasn't allowed to say what was really on my mind. My mom would interrupt and correct me, or hush me if she thought I was going to start talking about something she didn't want anyone to know about.

In her mind, she was protecting me. She was trying to make sure that nobody would take me away from her. But really, thinking about it, all she was doing was wasting her money, taking me to a therapist and then telling me to lie when I got there.

As I sit here, developing this grand scheme to get myself out of this hospital, I become saddened by what I am doing. Until my father's visit, when he told me to 'get out of here', I have been busy sitting and writing in my journal. I've been slowly coming to the realisation that the abuse I'd grown up watching wasn't my fault at all. Now, before I can even wrap my mind around the idea and begin to really explore it, my father has come along and basically told me to 'get out of here', regardless of whether I am better or not. Once again, my family is too busy being concerned about appearances, and again, I am going to suffer for it. Some things just don't change.

For a second I regret having called the ambulance, but instantly chase the thought from my mind with a firm shake of my head.

'No.' I say out loud. 'I don't want to die. I just want to feel better.'

It is obvious though, that I am going to have to do this on my own. The staff here can't or won't help me; my parents can't or won't help me, and neither can my friends.

I know that I can't stay in the hospital forever, but I had hoped to stay in for a week or two more, simply because, despite the cold and the dirty walls and the crappy food, I am fairly safe here. I am being encouraged to get better. I am not told what to say, or told to hide my feelings. I have started to become human here. That's a heck of a realisation.

Now, I am going to have to become my machine-self again. I am going to have to lie, exaggerate, and not feel, while pretending I *do* feel, in order to get out of here. I am going to have to become a *cookie cutter person*; which is what I call normal average everyday people.

The thought makes me queasy. I feel that all I have left is my individuality, and no amount of abuse or torment or mockery has taken that away from me. If anything, I have used the horrible circumstances of my family life to build the shield that protects me from the outside world. I am machine, something that cannot feel and cannot be hurt. Not like a *cookie cutter person*. At least that's what I'd thought.

I remain largely unconcerned with things that most *normal* girls my age are concerned with: make-up, labels and taking stupid quizzes out of teenage magazines to figure out if I am a good kisser or not. I feel superior to girls whose day is ruined if they get a zit on their usually flawless skin. Or if their hair doesn't turn out right any given day.

I am still busy throwing all of this around in my mind when I hear someone call for afternoon therapy.

'OK Emma,' I tell myself. 'Time to get out of here.' I smooth my hair, throw my shoulders back, and grab my journal. With a new sense of purpose, I walk down the hall, ready for therapy.

CHAPTER 12
Try to be convincing

I take my seat in group therapy, telling myself that all I have to do is act normal and nice, and after a few days, everything will be OK. If I can just figure out what *normal* is...

Instead of Dr X walking in though, another man in a white coat comes in and introduces himself as Dr Murphy. I frown. Dr X is who I need to convince to let me out of the hospital, not this other mystery doctor. I tap my fingers anxiously on my knees as I wait for everyone to finish shuffling papers and changing seats, so they can sit by their *friends* in here. I shake my head. Even in a mental hospital, it's still like high school. I don't even fit in with the *crazy* people.

The session starts. It takes a great deal more effort than I initially thought it would to try to keep my usual, disdainful expression from my face. It's particularly difficult when I have to listen to things I don't consider important. For example, almost anything to do with anyone else my age.

I remind myself of my newfound goal though, and I try hard to listen to everyone else as they talk, and keep my attention from turning inward.

It gets to be my turn in this circle-jerk pity party, and I begin a semi-rehearsed diatribe of woe-is-me teenage angst over my parents' divorce. Even though I didn't care about it much in the first place, and I certainly don't care about it now. I need *something* to talk about, because I just want to get the hell out of this place.

I don't even really listen to what I'm saying, I'm just copying a lot of what the other patients were saying — how I want to live, how I am just depressed about my family and I don't know how to deal with it, blah blah blah. Everyone seems to buy it, and Dr Murphy makes notes and approving grunts. Thankfully, my turn passes and I breathe an inward sigh of relief. One down, eight more of these to go, I tell myself. I'm planning on it taking about seventy two hours to undo the damage I had done initially when I got here, with that whole tree-throwing incident.

I catch myself crossing my arms and scowling midway through one girl's speech about her third suicide attempt. It's unbearable when she starts to talk about how she didn't have any friends at school, and how that was her major depressive trigger. And then she starts sobbing, can you believe it? She's sobbing because she's not popular. Give me strength!

Remembering my plan, I change my expression to one of *faux* concern and uncross my arms, despite the fact I think she's a shallow moron. I'm unsure what to do with my arms, so I end up just folding my hands neatly in my lap. My toes trace circles on the floor with nervous energy.

Dr Murphy asks everyone to brainstorm *constructive ideas on dealing with stress* in response to this girl's question on how to deal with stress.

Almost everyone volunteers a thought, most of them taken from the generic list of ideas on our nearly identical treatment plans – you know, the pieces of paper that say dumb shit about gardening and calling your friends if you're feeling upset or stressed out or suicidal that day.

I panic when I realise I can't think of something that someone hasn't already said, and it's my turn to give a suggestion. And since I'm not in a waking coma, or too drugged out to answer, Dr Murphy expects a contribution from me.

Think Emma, think... What do normal people do? *Cookie cutter people.*

'Uh, play with your dog,' I finally blurt out.

A snicker escapes Ricky's lips and he

quickly tries to hide it as a cough when Dr Murphy's head snaps towards him, glaring at him for laughing at me. Ricky continues to pretend-cough, and even starts to pat his chest until Dr Murphy seems satisfied that he is not laughing at me.

The predictably lame group session ends. I'm sweating. Is it really *that* hard for me to act like a normal person? Then I notice that everyone else is pushing up their sleeves and fanning themselves with their journals. I gather that for once, instead of it being freezing cold in here, the heater must be working. I am relieved to discover that I haven't looked weird or awkward to everyone else.

Ricky comes and sits next to me. 'Play with puppies?' he asks, and laughs at me.

I scowl at him, not appreciating his sense of humour and cross my arms. 'No. I *said* play with your *dog*.'

'Oh come on Emma. What was that all about?'

'Uh, well, I decided after talking to my father today that I should, um, start trying to get better.'

Ricky's eyes widen. 'Dude, your *dad* came here?'

Aw crap, I think to myself when I realise that he's going to keep asking questions. The only reason I'm letting this conversation even start is in the hope that the staff will notice I'm conversing with other patients and write it up in their notes.

'Yes Ricky, he came by,' I say, already bored.

'Well? How'd it go?' he asks, settling into his chair like he's hoping for the lengthy explanation that I just won't give him.

'It went fine. We uh, ya know, hashed some stuff out and everything is OK.'

Ricky eyes me suspiciously. 'And that's it?'

'Yup. That's it,' I answer, nodding for greater effect.

Ricky decides to test my story. 'OK, well, what did you guys talk about?'

'Stuff,' I tell him. We glare at each other like gunfighters from the old West, and I realise that now we're in some sort of stupid staring contest. Perhaps Ricky imagines that somehow he is going to be able to make me tell him the truth. I smirk.

Ricky is not going to win this; I've perfected the art of the staring contest. In life, most people don't actually look you in the eye, and it makes them uncomfortable when someone does it to them.

Ricky finally concedes, as I knew he would. 'Fine then. Don't tell me,' he says, and storms off.

Left blissfully alone, my thoughts switch from getting out of the hospital, to my mom and step-dad. What have they told my friends about me?

I think back to the night I tried to kill myself. I remember very vaguely the fire trucks with their flashing sirens, and the ambulances, and the swarm of people who descended upon the house, intent on saving me from myself.

I live in a small town, on a small street, and news tends to travel fast in places like that. I know that everyone who knows me, knows my family, and hell, even those who didn't know *any* of us, will have heard hints, rumours, and allegations.

I feel suddenly bad. What kind of hell is Mom going through? No wonder she's embarrassed by me. She has tried so hard after the divorce to appear normal to everyone, and here I am, a daughter who refuses to conform, who is depressed all the time, and finally tried to kill herself.

Is everyone looking at them like they are bad parents? Have they gone back to work? I suddenly see Mom, hopelessly crying on the couch, unable to go back to her job out of sorrow and sheer embarrassment.

What about my step-dad, a man who married a woman with two kids, so poor they could barely feed themselves? He has never complained about inheriting kids with some severe emotional issues. He has really tried hard to be understanding, even though he can never grasp what we've been through. And this is how I am repaying him.

Another thought hits me. I am worried that the insurance won't pay for this, and somehow my parents will have to come up with thousands of dollars to cover my selfish stint in this hospital.

I can't blame everything on my parents. I am old enough to reason, to drive a car, to make choices for myself. I *chose* to try to end my life, because I chose *not* to confront my problems and get beyond them. I'm not sure how exactly I was supposed to deal with my problems. Nobody in my family had wanted to admit that there ever *was* a problem.

I am starting to get very nervous about leaving this place. Do my parents still love me? What kind of restrictions are going to be placed on me when I get out of here?

I sigh to myself when I realise that my panicked, worried parents are going to put me under a very close watch. I can pretty much rule out any sort of social life whatsoever, for God only knows how long. And then there is my father...

Will he want to be an active part of my life, now that I have threatened to take it? Is he guilt-stricken the way Mom most likely is? Does the thought even cross his mind that he had anything to do with this? Does he ever actually feel anything at all? *Ever*?

Now I feel irritated with myself; instead of focusing on *my* feelings, and how the events of the past were poisoning *me*, I am more concerned with how everyone else is.

Slowly but surely I am starting to see past the years of brainwashing that goes on when you grow up in an abusive home. And one of the biggest games that had been played with my mind was to have me grow up thinking that everything was my fault.

I was told, over and over, that if I was only smarter, faster, prettier, better behaved, less selfish, that my mom wouldn't get hit. And that I wouldn't *deserve* to be hit.

I can see so clearly right now; no child ever deserves to go through all that. Something has clicked inside me, and I can feel a sense of righteous anger building up in me.

OK, fine. I am going to get out of here, because this place is a goddamned joke. I am already at the point where I know what is going to be said in this group therapy session or that one, and in the counselling sessions. I have nothing more to learn from these people.

I'm not bitter. Everyone here means well. This place has been like a safety net for me. It has allowed me time to explore my inner feelings, and Dr X has encouraged me – you could say he's forced me – to deal with the past. And these are all great things, really, so I'm grateful in a way.

But the biggest issue for me to confront is something that no group therapy session will ever help with. I am going to have to be honest with my parents.

So I have made a decision. I am not going to let myself be manipulated any more. No one will make me blame myself for what my mom went through, or for whatever caused my father to become abusive in the first place.

I have also made a decision. When I get out of here, after my parents are done screaming, yelling, crying, or grounding me (or maybe even all of those things), I am going to sit them down. I am finally going to be honest with them and tell them exactly what caused me to feel like I had to end my life. If I have to face the past, then they are going to have to, too.

CHAPTER 13
The wrong doctor

I sit in Dr X's office, waiting for him to show up for our appointment. As I wait, I draw intricate spirals on a blank page in my journal.

At last the door opens. To my surprise Dr Murphy hurries in. I am shocked and disappointed and don't try to hide the fact.

Dr Murphy walks around to Dr X's desk and sits in his chair. I am irritated by his assumption of that chair; the one that belongs to *my* doctor, not to him.

Dr Murphy has my file, and begins to explain that Dr X isn't here today because of a family emergency. I start to tune him out, but doing that isn't going to help my case. I take a deep breath and calm myself.

Dr Murphy goes through a series of questions, checking them off as he asks them. He writes short notes underneath the questions, 'to give to Dr X, later'.

I can reply to most of the questions with short answers. Are you feeling suicidal today? No. How are you sleeping? Fine. Are you having any problems with your medications? No. Are you following your treatment plan? Yes. Do you have any questions about your treatment plan? No.

After about ten minutes, without even looking at me, Dr Murphy ends the session. I walk out of the office confused, and to be honest, kind of hurt. I watch a string of patients go in and out of that door the way I did. I feel slighted by the way that man has treated me. Like I am just another thing to deal with on his list of daily chores.

I remember how my father had done that to me when I was growing up, and how much it had hurt me. Half the time, when he talked to me, I warranted so little of his attention that he didn't even look up at me. Dr Murphy had inadvertently done the same thing to me in our session.

Logic tells me that he has most likely been thrown into doing the individual counselling sessions at the last minute. That still doesn't make me feel better though. Just as it hadn't made me feel better when my mom had tried to defend my father's constant dismissal of me as a child.

I feel horribly, inexplicably alone all of a sudden, even though I am in a room full of people. I remember the pay phone in the hallway, and picking up my journal I walk over to it. My heart races as I stare at the phone. Since I'm not allowed to have my cell phone in here, I can't remember any of my friends' phone numbers. I try to think of someone I can call.

I pick up the phone and carefully dial

the only phone number I can remember. The phone rings and rings. Eventually, the familiar voice of my mother comes down the line.

'Hi, I'm not in right now. Please leave a message and I'll get back to you.' The machine beeps for me to leave a message, but a lump has come to my throat, and I don't dare speak for fear of crying. I hang up the receiver and walk back, head down, to the group room.

I watch the frenzy of activity around me – people scurrying here and there, to the bathroom, to the doctor's office, to get something from their room, to rifle through magazines and old books with missing pages on the beaten-up bookshelf. Desperate, I look for Ricky and find him, playing draughts with some kid whose name I don't know.

I start to feel very sorry for myself. I remember going to school as a kid and how I could never seem to make many friends, or keep the ones I did make. Kids do stupid things to each other, like get into fights and call each other names. But for some reason I considered all of these things acts of treachery that should not go unpunished. I ended up isolating myself then, just as I have done here. The truth is though, I don't actually *like* anyone in this place. It's just that right now, I don't want to be alone. I am exhausted; tired of thinking, tired of pretending, tired of trying to trick people, and so *very* tired of the thoughts warring inside my brain.

I have a very bad headache that has come on quickly. I close my eyes and rub the bridge of my nose with my thumb and forefinger. I stop when I recall that I've seen Dr X do the same thing. I feel betrayed by him not being here for me today. I know that he has to have some sort of life outside of the hospital, but I just expected that Dr X would be there, working with me until I left. Now I am worrying that he won't be. It's a juvenile thought, but a genuine worry.

I have a curious mix of fear, revulsion and respect for Dr X. He has seen through me and demanded that I give him the truth.

And I have argued with him, lied to him, and resented him for making me be honest with myself as well as him. I resent him for bringing up the past and for making me deal with it.

Now I'm blaming Dr X for the way I am; stuck in here, isolated from everyone. I'm muttering to myself. Stupid doctor with his stupid speeches about getting well. I'm not really making any sense but still feel better, complaining about Dr X and blaming my current state on him. In the end I let out a long sigh. I know I can't blame Dr X for me being in this state. I'm just sulking.

After a while I tire of being alone with myself and walk over to the nurses' desk. I ask for drawing supplies and after a few moments get a plastic box filled with crayons, pastels and a few pencils. I sit in a chair, next to the dirty cruddy windows with the steel inside them, trying to figure out what to draw. I frown. Nothing inspires me in here. I look out of the window again, and suddenly breathe in sharply. The sun is shining through a wet, leafless tree, in the middle of the courtyard. I have never noticed this tree before, since right across the courtyard is another wing of this hospital and usually I am trying to peer through the windows to see what's going on over there.

The tree looks almost black, and its branches, bare and almost skeletal, stretch up and out, towards the sun. I silently thank the tree for being there, and I grab a pencil from the box. I'm going to draw that tree.

I spend most of the afternoon sketching the tree, using swift strokes of the soft pastels to show more of the contrast between the darkness of the tree, and the green of the soggy grass around it. Finally, I stare at my picture. I frown. It sucks. It looks nothing like the beautiful tree outside. That tree, despite being bare and stripped down, seems to be reaching out for sunlight to a sky that has granted only rain for days.

I admire that tree and consider it my kin. That tree has probably struggled through dry seasons, and too much rain, and been stripped down by the seasons of life, but is still standing. And still reaching for the light.

OK, so maybe I'm not an artist, but I *can* write, and I want to get that thought down. I tuck the crappy drawing of the tree inside of my journal and flip to a blank page.

December ??

So I was trying to draw this tree outside, and as I looked at it, something came to me.

This tree was beautiful. Even though it has been through the ups and downs of life, it is still standing, feet firmly rooted in the ground, and reaching for the light.

This sounds stupid, and I know it, but I want to be like that tree. I want to be able to weather the storms of life, and to keep reaching for light, even though right now I feel like I'm stripped bare, with nothing of me left.

So even though I'm sitting in a hospital right before Christmas, and I'm alone, I will look at the ugly ass picture I tried to draw of the beautiful tree, and remember how that tree was still standing, despite everything.

I turn to another page in my journal and, inspired by the tree, I realise that I don't have any hobbies that don't involve minor infractions of the law. Drinking, ditching school and having sex aren't considered healthy hobbies. Let's face it; they're not hobbies at all. But they have been my only interests.

I remember the generic list in one of the leaflets, of *healthy activities* to do if you get stressed out after you are discharged from the hospital. I decide to make up one of my own. The problem is, I can't really think of anything that I want to do. So I try to think about what I am at least *interested* in.

Music. I love music. I spent hours listening to it when I wasn't in this place. Suddenly, I want to listen to music so badly that I feel like crying. I sigh, and sadly write the word *music* under my list of hobbies that I want to pursue when I get out of here.

I chew on my pencil, deep in thought. I am really, *really,* having a hard time figuring out what I enjoy doing. I note with some sadness that I can't remember the last time I really enjoyed anything. It is almost as if I've existed behind a plate of glass, watching other people live and laugh and feel, and being incapable of doing it myself. *That's what machines do. Machines do lots of things, but they don't feel.*

A new fear overtakes me, one that I can honestly say I can't remember feeling before. *What if I can't change? What if this is how I will always be? I've turned myself into a machine, but can I turn myself back? Can I become a human again?*

I am suddenly very worried that I am going to be stuck this way – miserable, alone, unhappy, and incapable of feeling much of anything. I think about the meds I am on, and realise that I've come to appreciate them for the sense of calm they are giving me. Am I just trying to drug myself so that I don't feel anything? Isn't that what the meds are designed to do after all?

I feel dizzy. Too many thoughts in my head and it's getting hard to breathe. Life suddenly seems to be a large, looming monster, one that I cannot deal with. Panic starts to overtake me as I begin to hyperventilate. Just as my erratic breathing is becoming noticeable to others, I happen to turn my head and notice the tree.

I make the slightest whimpering noise at the sight of it standing there, and I remember. I remember that the tree stands, despite the storms that it has weathered. My breathing slows back to normal, and I just focus on that tree until I feel calm again.

OK Emma. You're OK. Everything is going to be OK. You're going to be like the tree, Emma, I tell myself. I whisper so that I don't look like a total weirdo to anyone who might be watching.

The Finer Points of Becoming...

You're going to be just fine. You're going to get through this. If the tree is still standing, you can do the same thing...

It doesn't quite make sense; not in a linear, logical, *machine* sort of way, my fascination with this tree. But in a very *human* sort of way, my newfound love for the tree does make sense. I really *am* going to be like that tree.

I smile to myself. I, a *machine,* have fallen in love with a tree. I laugh softly when I think how silly it sounds, but it makes me happy. I have found something that makes sense to me, sets an example for me to follow. And even if it's just a tree, well, I like that. I have at least begun to think like a human again.

CHAPTER 14
'All good things…'

December ??

I don't deserve to live and breathe and feel. I ruin everything I touch.

So begins my journal entry this morning. I woke up in a foul mood, for reasons I am unsure of. I think it is a combination of mental and physical exhaustion, plus the fact that I woke, shivering, before the lights were on. The heating had gone off again.

Once again the familiar cycle of wake, shower, go to the main room, eat, take meds, and sit through group therapy has started. I am beginning to understand why anyone who has been in here for any length of time has turned into what I call a *zombie*. This place drains the life out of you; it is even becoming a chore to move. Certainly, it is taking much more energy than I had thought it would to pretend that everything is *OK,* and that I am doing *better*.

Truth be told, even though I have enjoyed the protective environment that being in the hospital has offered, that feeling has grown old and stale. I want my clothes back; I want my make-up and – most of all – I want my music back.

I sit in the chair, waiting for my meeting with Dr X. Well, I hope it will be Dr X, not the other doctor who had casually dismissed me yesterday. If it is going to be Dr X, he is late – it is ten past our meeting time and still he isn't here.

Just as I start to think that the meeting is going to be cancelled, Dr X rushes in, dropping files and folders along the way.

'Goddammit!' he says loudly, and I jump

in the chair, startled.

I help him pick up the files and folders, and carry them to his desk.

'Thank you, Emma,' he says to me, and hopelessly pushes the assortment of papers to one side of his desk. I assume he'll sort through them later.

He opens my file and takes a few minutes to read it. I sit across from him, on my hands to keep them warm, swinging my legs. I notice the picture of his family and remember that he hadn't been here yesterday because of a family emergency. I am suddenly worried about them, for some unknown reason.

'Hey Dr X, um, is everything OK?' I ask him.

He looks up at me, startled. 'Huh?' he says back. He hasn't heard what I said.

'They told me you weren't here yesterday because of an emergency. Is everything OK?'

The Finer Points of Becoming...

Recognition crosses his face and Dr X half smiles at me. 'Everything is fine, my wife slipped in the shower and bumped her head pretty badly. Thanks for asking, Emma.'

I smile back and wait for him to finish reading. I suddenly become nervous and hope that Dr Murphy has said good things about me. I start to chew on my fingernails.

Dr X raises his eyebrows in surprise as he reads. I can only guess at what is written in my file. After what seems like an eternity, he looks up at me.

'Well. Seems you're doing much better, Emma. You're participating more in group sessions, focusing on your treatment plan, writing in your journal, doing your classwork. That's very good.'

He pauses and adjusts his glasses before his gaze turns razor sharp, so that it seems to cut right through me.

I know what he is doing. He is trying to see if I'm faking. I politely smile as our eyes meet.

'So, Emma. How are you feeling?'

For a split second, I want to tell Dr X about the meeting with my father, and how my father had told me to say and do whatever I had to do to get out of here. But I don't.

'I'm doing a lot better, Doc. Really trying to, uh, you know, deal with my issues and stuff.'

As soon as the words come out of my mouth, I want to kick myself. I'm not speaking with the poise and grace that I have practised.

Dr X continues to look straight at me. He leans back in his chair and taps his pen on the desk. He seems to be mulling something over.

'Well, that's very good,' he says at last. 'What do you think is helping you feel better?'

I open my mouth to speak then think better of it. I hadn't really planned for this question. I haven't been expecting it. Damn him.

'Well, I think the medication is helping. I've been eating more, which, um, is helping. And I've been sleeping better, so that's good too. Um, I also talked to both of my parents, and they're very supportive of me and are going to help me when I get out of here.'

Dr X doesn't move. I'm not sure if I've messed up or not. I freeze beneath his icy stare.

'You've talked to *both* of your parents,' he says. I think I know where he is going with this.

'Yes. My father came to visit me the other day.'

'Yes, I know Emma. How did that go?'

Again, it occurs to me that I should tell the truth. That I am confused about my father; that I don't know what to think, and that I feel like a jerk for trying to kill myself and embarrassing my family. But, I didn't say any of that. I just tell Dr X what I think he wants to hear.

'We both decided that we should let go of the past and start a new relationship together. He says that he wants to support me when I get out of here and spend more time with me.'

'And is that OK with you, Emma?' Dr X asks. He makes little notes in my file as we talk.

'Yep,' I say.

Dr X considers my answer. Then he flips through my chart and begins to re-read it. He's taking his time, reading and re-reading stuff, and making little notes. What the hell is he doing?

Dr X looks at me again, and sighs. 'Well Emma, it would *appear* that you are doing better. The nurses, orderlies and other hospital staff have made notes to that effect. You're co-operating more, and you're becoming more social as well.'

Dr X paused for effect.

'However, I must admit I am slightly suspicious of this sudden turn for the better.'

He pauses again. I can't move. I want to scream. Instead, I'm just sitting here, silently. Dr X continues.

'As a general rule it takes more than just a few days for a patient to show the level of change that your progress reports are suggesting. Makes me wonder...'

Dr X pauses again. It's clear that there's more he wants to say, but he just sighs and shakes his head. Eventually he continues.

'The fact is, I cannot keep you here based on just a hunch, Emma. I've already spoken with both of your parents, and they do seem very supportive of you, and more than willing to continue to help you with your treatment plan when you get out of the hospital.'

Dr X watches me, looking for a reaction. I don't have much of one. I'm not quite sure what Dr X is saying. One minute he seems to be implying that he doesn't believe me, the next minute he says that he can't keep me here. I'm confused, to say the least.

'Do you understand what I'm telling you Emma?' Dr X asks.

I shake my head. 'No. I don't.'

Dr X nods. 'I'm sure this must be very confusing for you Emma. What I'm trying to tell you is that *personally* I think you should stay here a little bit longer. However, according to hospital protocol, you are ready to be discharged.'

I'm sitting very still, not moving. Dr X notices my lack of movement and continues to spell out to me what he's saying.

'Emma. I can't keep you here any longer.'

I feel like a rush of cold air has hit me. I shiver as I take a deep, long breath. And I just can't help myself. I smile.

Dr X doesn't return my smile however, so I quickly stop.

'Off the record, Emma, I'm very concerned about you. I know you haven't been honest with me since you've been here. I have my ideas as to why you hide your true self away, but I cannot prove anything. I really mean this in a nice way, Emma, but I hope I never see you again.'

I frown when Dr X says he doesn't want to see me again, before I realise what he actually means. He isn't stupid, he has seen through my act. But I'm not throwing trees at anyone or refusing to co-operate, so he's powerless to do much of anything to keep me from leaving the hospital. And when he says he doesn't want to see me again, it's just because if he does, it most likely means that I have tried to kill myself again. He really *does* mean it in a nice way.

'I understand Doc. You won't see me again.'

Our eyes meet, and he's sending me an unspoken message. Something along the lines of *I know that you know that I know that you're still screwed up, and I'm trying to tell you to take care of yourself.* I want to laugh because that sounds like a line from some stupid comedy show or something, but I just nod quietly. Dr X nods back at me. He knows that he's got his point across.

Dr X breaks the silence. 'I am going to recommend you for discharge, Emma. If everything continues to go well, your parents can most likely pick you up tomorrow morning. I will speak to them today and inform them of your progress and our intent to discharge you. You just take good care of yourself, Emma.'

I am suddenly aware of the fact that I am going to miss Dr X very much. My eyes begin to tear up. I am confused. I should be very happy, but instead I am afraid. And sad.

Dr X smiles to reassure me. 'You're as tough as nails, Emma. You'll be fine.'

I can't talk. A lump is forming in my throat. I swallow hard and run a hand through my hair. And straighten my back. I am *not* going to cry.

'Thanks for everything Doc,' I say, getting to my feet.

Dr X is already sorting through the stack of papers on his desk. He looks up at me. 'You're welcome, Emma. You can go now.'

I feel I want to say something else to him, but I don't really know what. In the end though, I keep it simple.

'Bye Doc,' I say. And that's it. That's all I can find to say to the man who has probably helped me more than anyone else in my whole life. Even so, I think Dr X understands what I am trying to say. I look at him and realise how tired he is. I'm suddenly more grateful than ever for having met him.

'Goodbye Emma,' Dr X answers. And then he's back to his mountain of paperwork, getting ready for the next patient.

I walk calmly to the bathroom and as soon as the door is shut behind me, I start to cry. I'm crying because I am afraid, and because I've never been very good at goodbyes. And this goodbye is permanent. It has to be.

Slowly, my tears stop. Excitement begins to well up in my chest as I remember that I am getting the hell out of here. I smile and giggle to myself. It dawns on me that I have been in the bathroom for quite some time, so I quickly wash my face to erase any evidence of tears that might still remain.

When I walk back to the group room, Ricky walks over to me and sits down. It's OK though; not even Ricky's constant but well-meaning pestering can bother me right now.

'Well you look chipper today. What's going on Emma?' he asks.

A smile stretches from ear to ear across my face, and I know that I am going to be OK. I am tough as nails. I am going to make it.

'I'm going home Ricky.'

CHAPTER 15
Endgame

My mom and I are arguing. I think this one started over my refusal to wear clothing in any colour other than black. I'm sitting on the bathroom floor and crying, with my head in my hands. My mom has hit me, and she tried to get me to hit her back. My refusal to do so has only angered her even more. I know she's going to twist the story to make it sound like it's my fault. She's screaming at me and I have my hands clamped over my ears to muffle the sound.

'What do you want Emma? What do you want? Do you want to go live with your father? I CAN'T DO THIS ANY MORE WITH YOU!'

I stop crying like a switch has been flipped. Very calmly, I lock eyes with my mother and I say what I need to say in a single simple sentence.

'If you send me to live with that abusive asshole again, I am going to kill myself...'

I wake up and frown. Why in the hell have I dreamt about *that* argument with my mom? I'm not really angry about it – I knew she'd never send me to live with him, and I know she is frustrated because her daughter is a depressed mess. I didn't blame her for her reaction then. So why am I dreaming about it now?

I don't have much time to ponder the reason for this unpleasant reverie, because the lights are turned on and I begin the process of getting dressed. I shake off the memory as being just another nightmare and decide that I am *not* going to be in a bad mood today. Today is the day that I am going home and I am so excited I can barely stand it.

Of course, I am still nervous and unsure of what to expect when I get home. But whatever happens, it is bound to be better than being here. I mean, it *has* to be better than here, right?

I join everyone else in the main room and eat a breakfast that is just slightly warm – not burnt or rubbery for a change. I consider it to be a good omen, a sign that things *are* indeed changing. And for the better.

I am practically humming to myself when I get in line for my meds. The water feels cool in my mouth, not tepid like it usually is. Yet another good sign that things are going to start going my way.

I sit in my final group therapy session, and even talk about my excitement at getting out of the hospital. And what it will be like to begin rebuilding relationships with my family. And how I'm going to explore healthy, creative outlets for my emotions when I get out of here. And you know what? I'm not pretending. I am completely serious about trying to become a healthy, sane human being. I've had enough of being sick, tired, and most of all, *a machine.*

After group therapy, when everyone is busy waiting their turn to file into Dr X's office for their private therapy and assessments, a kindly nurse comes over to me. She explains that my parents are going to be picking me up at noon.

Excitedly, I go to my room to pack my few belongings into the plastic bag she's given me. Really, the only things I am taking are the Bible my father had given me and my journal. I think for a moment about *not* taking the journal, just throwing it away. But I decide against it. It is a testament to my decision to get better.

I finish packing and give the bag to the nurse. She takes it up to the front desk to hold for me until I am discharged from the hospital.

The last few hours before noon seem to drag by so slowly that at times it feels like the clock isn't moving at all.

At noon I am called to the front desk, where my mom is waiting for me. I smile, run up to her and hug her. She hugs me back, but it doesn't feel quite the way I remembered. I frown. She feels a little stiff and uncomfortable. She's never hugged me like that before. Or have I just been in here for so long that I have forgotten? God, is she mad at me for some reason? A twinge of nervousness runs through me, settling in my stomach.

'Hi Mom,' I say, and it comes out almost like a question. To my relief, she doesn't seem angry at me. Maybe a little sad, but not angry.

'Hi Emma. Let's get you home, OK?' she says. She brushes my cheek softly with the back of a finger. For once, I don't care if anyone sees me being affectionate with my mom. In fact, I desperately *want* people to see it. Then they will see that I am loved, and that I am not a freak.

My mom has brought a change of clothes for me. I go back to my room to strip out of the hospital clothing and slip into something that is more, well, *me.*

My mom has brought me a black t-shirt, my favorite black hoodie sweatshirt and sneakers and blue jeans. I frown. Where in the *hell* had she found blue jeans that belonged to me? I don't even remember ever *owning* a pair of blue jeans. But still, it's better than the hospital clothing that I'm tearing off at lightspeed.

I dress in record time and run down the hall, throwing the dirty clothes in the laundry bin in the hallway. *Good riddance,* I mutter as I toss them in, running back up the hallway to meet with my mom again. She is busy signing my discharge paperwork.

I see the nurse hand her a folder of paperwork and a brown paper bag with my meds in it. The nurse is explaining what I am taking and how often. My mom glances at me briefly, just the once, and when she does, she wears an expression that I can't identify. Is she ashamed of me? I begin to chew on my fingers. I am anxious, just wanting to get the hell out of here. Suddenly I am overcome with a feeling that I am *never* going to leave this place; that this is all some elaborate trick, and that my mom is going to leave without me.

At last, when I can stand it no longer, the nurse is done talking, and my mom picks up the folder and the bag. My mom hands the bag to me.

'Hold these Emma,' she says, all matter-of-fact. I peer up at her suspiciously. This is just not like her.

'Mom, why are you acting weird? Do you still love me?' I ask her quietly.

My mom stops walking and looks me square in the eyes. 'Emma, I will *always*, *always* love you. That will never change, OK? I've just had a rough week too.'

I feel only slightly relieved, because now I feel guilty as hell. I sigh and carry on walking down the hallway, next to my mom.

We walk out of the building, towards the parking lot. When we get to the car, I stop and turn to look back at the hospital. Then, I look up at the sky. There are some clouds, but there are beautiful streaks of blue, breaking up the monotony of the grey. I look to the distance and see dark storm clouds rolling slowly towards us.

My mom interrupts my thoughts. 'Come on, Emma. It's supposed to rain again, and I want to get home before the weather gets too bad.'

I get into the car. We drive home with the radio on, so neither of us has to talk. I fidget, nervously. Finally, I can't stand the silence between us any more.

'I'm sorry Mom. Please don't hate me,' I blurt out.

'Emma, I *don't* hate you honey. Please stop saying that. Just... you need to understand... that this is going to take some time to get over. And things are going to be different when you get home.'

I had known that when I finally made it out of the hospital that things *were* going to be different. In most ways I am ready and waiting for them to be different. But I am still afraid. I remember Dr X's words to me when he had sensed the fear inside me at our last meeting. 'You're as tough as nails, Emma,' he'd said. I smile a little bit, despite myself. I tell myself that everything is going to be OK, and not to be afraid.

'How's Rosemary?' I ask my mother.

My mom hesitates for a split second before she answers. 'She's fine. She's at a friend's house right now.'

I am slightly pissed off that my sister isn't at home for me to see, but I won't be making a scene about it.

Mom says she has to make a stop, and pulls into the car park of the off-licence at the bottom of the hill, before you come up to our house.

'Wait here,' she says. She comes back a

few minutes later with a bottle of wine in a brown paper bag.

We drive the rest of the way home in silence. I don't know exactly what I had been expecting, but I had hoped that she would be, I don't know, maybe excited to have me back home? It sounds silly I know, but I had been *so* excited to get home myself that I had wanted to find at least a *little* of that mirrored in my mom. But what I'm picking up on seems to be... what? Anxiety? Fear? Whatever it is, I can't quite place it.

I am beginning to make myself a nervous wreck before I finally decide that things cannot be rushed. Healing is going to take time.

We hit the gravel in the driveway and the sound jerks me out of my thoughts. Before the car even stops, I have unbuckled my seatbelt and I run up to the house. I pull up the mat on the front porch, and discover that the key I usually use to get into the house isn't there.

'Hey Mom, where's the key?' I ask.

My mom doesn't say anything at all. She just unlocks the door herself. I am starting to get creeped-out by my mom's behaviour.

My mom goes into the kitchen and I follow on behind her. She opens the bottle of wine, pours herself a glass, and quickly downs the whole thing. She has still not said a word.

'Um. I'm going to go to my room now Mom.' I say.

My words seem to hover in the air, and my mom simply pours herself another glass of wine.

I walk through the house that is as silent as a tomb. I stop off at the door of Rosemary's room, hoping that she'd come home from her friend's house. Rosemary is not there. I sigh and continue walking down the hall, until I get to my bedroom.

I open the door, and my heart stops. Unable to believe what I am seeing, I run back down the hallway into the kitchen. My mother is still silent as a statue, drinking her wine.

'Mom, what the hell did you do to my room? Where's all my stuff? Mom?'

I had opened the door to my room to find it an empty space. No posters, no pictures, no clothes in the closet, and not a stick of furniture in it. It is like I had never existed.

'MOM!' I finally shout. Slowly, like it is taking a great effort, her head turns towards me. Her hazel eyes finally meet mine. There is not a shred of emotion in them, and I realise that *that* was what I had been unable to identify in my mom at the hospital. And during the ride home. She was cold... no, not just cold... *mechanical*.

When my mother finally does speak, she speaks calmly and flatly, as efficient as any judge handing out a sentence to a condemned prisoner.

'I told you, things were going to change when you got home, Emma.'

'OK, so what the hell does that have to do with where my stuff is Mom?' I yell at her. I am afraid. Truly afraid. I have *never* seen my mom act like this.

My mother calmly continues. 'I'm sorry, Emma,' she says, pausing to pour herself another glass of wine. I just watch her drinking, stunned. Finally, I remember that I can speak.

'Sorry for *what* Mom? Did you throw my shit away?'

My mother's eyes meet mine, and though there is still not a shred of emotion in them, a single tear runs down her cheek.

'Emma. I can't do this any more. I'm sorry. You're too much for me to handle.'

I listen to her and can't believe what I am hearing. 'So what the hell does that mean, Mom?'

My mother finishes her glass of wine and turns her back to me. Outside, sloppy wet drops of rain smack loudly on the car, on the pavement, over everything. My mother and I stand in the rapidly darkening kitchen in silence. Finally, I can handle it no more.

'Mom, what the *hell* are you saying?' I yell in frustration.

'Emma, I packed your things and sent them to your father's house.'

'Well what the hell would you do *that* for?' I ask, not understanding – *refusing* to understand – what she is saying.

'Because Emma, you're going to live there.'

I don't say anything. Just what can I say to that? I stare at her and she just keeps lifting that glass of wine to her lips, regular as clockwork, like she's a machine. It's funny that I had never seen it before. My mom as a machine. Through my frustration and fear, I'm beginning to see that perhaps just about anyone can become a machine. You just have to have the need to shut the world out.

But then I wonder, has my mom always been a machine and I've been so busy becoming a machine myself that I just never noticed? That could explain a lot about me. Perhaps it takes a machine to breed a machine.

I don't even want to think about it as I reach down deep within myself to find the switch that hides there in the darkness. If I'm going to survive, I'd better power up.